LOVE MARRIAGE

CEYLON

LOVE MARRIAGE

a novel

V. V. GANESHANANTHAN

RANDOM HOUSE
TRADE PAPERBACKS
New York

Love Marriage is a work of fiction. Names, characters, places, and incidents are the products of the author's imagination or are used fictitiously. Any resemblance to actual events, locales, or persons, living or dead, is entirely coincidental.

A Random House Trade Paperback Original

Title page map courtesy of antiqueprints.com

Published in the United States by Random House Trade Paperbacks, an imprint of The Random House Publishing Group, a division of Random House, Inc., New York.

RANDOM HOUSE TRADE PAPERBACKS and colophon are trademarks of Random House, Inc.

RANDOM HOUSE READER'S CIRCLE and colophon are trademarks of Random House, Inc.

LIBRARY OF CONGRESS CATALOGING-IN-PUBLICATION DATA

Ganeshananthan, V. V.
Love marriage : a novel / V.V. Ganeshananthan.
p. cm.
ISBN 978-1-4000-6669-8 (trade pbk.)
1. Sri Lankan Americans—Social life and customs—Fiction. 2. Family—Fiction.
3. Intergenerational relations—Fiction. 4. Tamil (Indic people)—Social conditions—Fiction. I. Title.
PS3607.A455L68 2008
813'.6—dc22 2007024120

Printed in the United States of America

www.randomhousereaderscircle.com

2 4 6 8 9 7 5 3 1

Book design by Barbara M. Bachman

for

AMMA, APPA, *and* DEVAN

Today we have naming of parts. Yesterday,
We had daily cleaning. And tomorrow morning,
We shall have what to do after firing. But today,
Today, we have naming of parts.

—from

NAMING OF PARTS,

Lessons of the War, Henry Reed

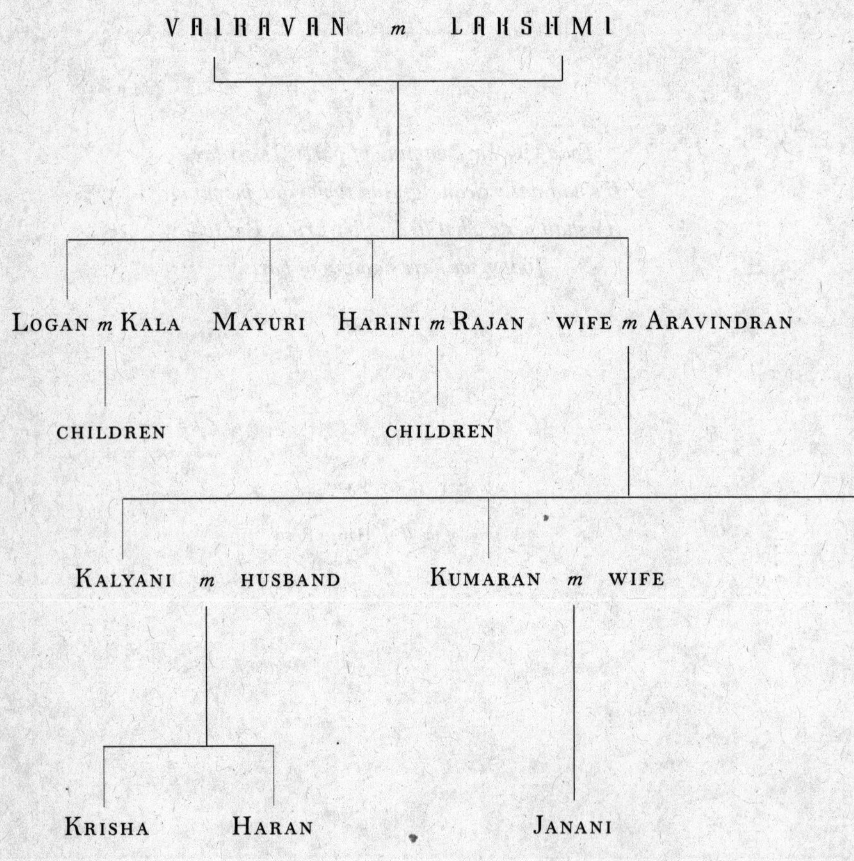
VAIRAVAN m LAKSHMI
LOGAN m KALA
MAYURI
HARINI m RAJAN
WIFE m ARAVINDRAN
CHILDREN
CHILDREN
KALYANI m HUSBAND
KUMARAN m WIFE
KRISHA
HARAN
JANANI

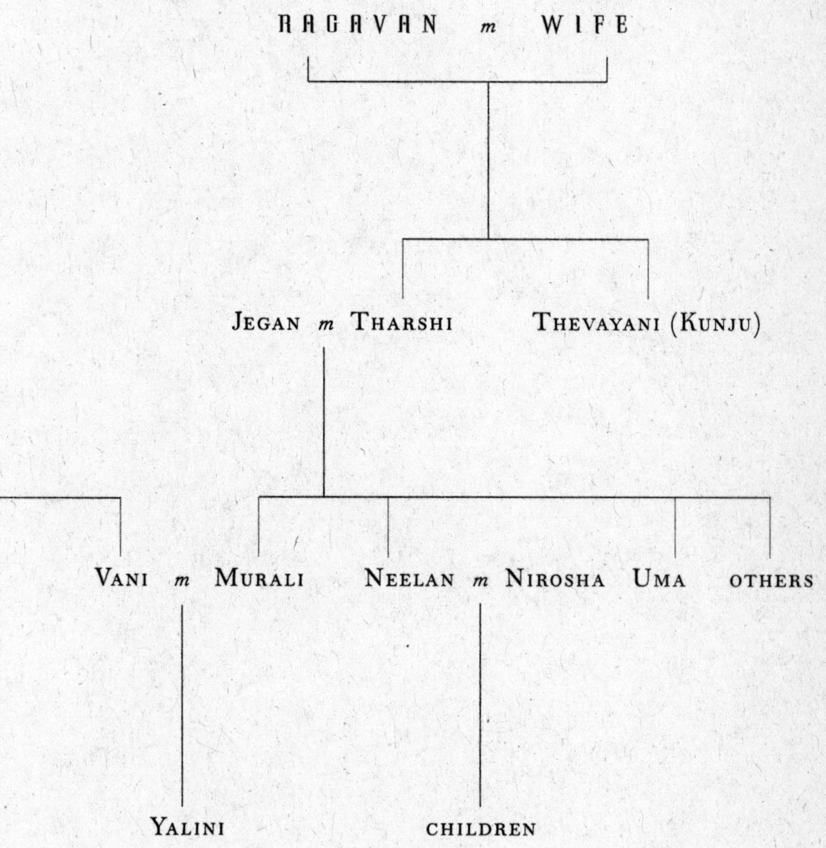

RAGAVAN m WIFE
JEGAN m THARSHI
THEVAYANI (KUNJU)
VANI m MURALI
NEELAN m NIROSHA
UMA
OTHERS
YALINI
CHILDREN

LOVE MARRIAGE

IN THIS GLOBE-SCATTERED SRI LANKAN FAMILY, WE SPEAK only of two kinds of marriage. The first is the Arranged Marriage. The second is the Love Marriage. In reality, there is a whole spectrum in between, but most of us spend years running away from the first toward the second.

Among the categories that bleed outside these two carefully delineated boundaries: the Self-Arranged Marriage, the Outside Marriage, the Cousin Marriage, the Village Marriage, the Marriage Abroad. There is the Marriage Without Consent. There is the Marriage Under Pressure. There is even Marrying the Enemy, who, it turns out, is not an Enemy at all.

You cannot go unfettered into a family's history if you are one of them. The nature of certain unions will be hidden from you, rephrased to you, the subject dropped, the music changed. There is Proper Marriage; there is Improper Marriage. This Tamil family speaks of the latter in whispers.

THE RULE IS THAT all families begin with a marriage. And the other way around.

You don't marry a person, my father says to no one in particular. You marry a family.

The Self-Arranged Marriage: my father has married my mother's family so successfully that he now fits into it as well as—if not better than—he fits into his own. My mother is an Aravindran and, further back than that, a Vairavan, which means that the members of her family—especially her siblings—are nosy, noisy, close, and concerned with domestic comforts. Years after they stopped living where they had always lived, in a small house in the village of Urelu, in the town of Jaffna, they remain connected by telephone lines and carefully written aerograms. They never forget birthdays, favorite curries, or unkindnesses. They were once three but are now two. My father loves my mother's family, and in return for that they draw him in. They have forgotten that when he wanted to marry my mother they circled around her protectively from the far corners of the globe, opposed to her marrying a man they had never even met. They only remember that she has a happy life in a country far safer than the one in which she was born.

And twenty-five years after their wedding, my parents like to give the impression that their marriage was Arranged, because they are both very Proper. But their secret is out: they fell in love. Those who are watching can see how in certain moments they become each other. This has been their way of falling in love: the acquisition of each other's habits, mannerisms, preferences, and witticisms. They have built a wall around their twoness, and each brick laid in place is a secret that only they share, or perhaps an exception one has made for the other. They have become an example of how you can Have Your Love and Eat It Too. They let everyone think that they took no responsibility for the way they came together. They engaged in all the dances of manners and the ceremonies involved in a Traditional Marriage, which is to say, an Arranged Marriage. This, they say, is not a romance. It begins with an introduction, a handshake, which is not the custom of the East but has become the greeting of the West. The touching of fingers is a strange, luscious intimacy, a preface to the story.

These two, my parents, have not acknowledged their secret—perhaps not even to each other. And they have exchanged rings and vows and hearts without eliciting the frowns that Improper Marriages frequently do.

MURALI: IT HAD ONCE been thought that the young doctor who would later become my father would not marry at all. He came from a family in Ariyalai, a village on the outskirts of Jaffna. And his was a family full of doctors, a family full of poor doctors with heart problems. His own murmured persistently; he was told he would not live past forty. *Don't exert yourself too much, young man.* He tempered any enthusiasm for sports, believing strenuous activity would shorten his life, moment by moment. He was last on the cricket field, first out of breath. In a family of five sisters and three brothers that was all too obsessed with Marriages (regardless of category), he decided—rather nobly—not to marry at all: he would only leave a husbandless woman like his mother. His schoolmates, with the canny cruelty of children, called him Hole-in-the-Heart.

Every year from the age of three, when the murmur was first discovered, he had his chest x-rayed so that they could check the size of his Heart. They were afraid that it was too big. This happened sometimes to children with murmurs, the whispers of childhood turning into an adult sickness. An enlarged heart. Later, as a doctor, he would ask for impromptu ultrasounds, echo cardiograms. *Sound out my heart. Please check to make sure it's still there. Do you see it?* He had grown into a scientist. He wanted to know that the blood would continue its flow through his veins, that his pulse would not stop without warning one day, like an alarm clock gone off not at its appointed hour, but years too early. He wanted to see the proof of his own life for himself. He listened to his own heart sometimes when he was alone, unbuttoning his shirt as though it was a gateway into his shallow chest. He slipped in and out of radiology rooms as he pleased, without appointments. Lying on his back, his doctor's coat open, he exposed the Heart that had betrayed him to the eye of radiation. No matter which method he used to see into his own body, he would always leave with an image in hand, his sweaty fingers holding the evidence of his own mortality. Weak-kneed because he was weakhearted.

Over the years, despite himself, he would imagine his own dying: how on his fortieth birthday he would suddenly look into some mirror and see death on a face that had always looked younger than it really was. He would be eating breakfast, or perhaps walking up the road to post a letter to his mother, and would crumble to his knees, his body collapsing limb by limb, the Heart slowing, and slowing, and slowing. The blood no longer flowing to his brain. The sound of a heart—his Heart—stopping.

He had a dream of being buried in a coffin of red lacquer, with a crowd of mourners wearing hats, singing and carrying pictures of him. In the dream he is passed from person to person like a torch. In this absolute stillness of death, he can sense himself traveling, moved by the hands of strangers. When the crowd of mourners reaches a bridge, the undertakers take the coffin from them and begin to run. The mourners cannot cross the bridge but watch him drift away from them. He is carried away into a distant, foggy death: A vagueness. An ending.

He wakes up. He is sweating. He is cold. As a Hindu, he will not be buried in a coffin. Someday, fire will find his body; a man of his family will hold the torch to the pyre. And then his ashes will find the sea. But as a young man, he cannot get rid of this body. It bears him up and holds him back.

MURALI: HE WAS THE first in his family to come to the United States. Sri Lankan doctors were well respected in the medical community there, if only because they were Asian. He had secured a position at a hospital in New England, where he would be a resident and complete his training. But it was not so easy to leave Jaffna, where he had grown up. He is not well, his relatives said to his mother, the widow. How can you send him away? His mother, Tharshi, feeling guilty and thinking that she should not let him go, asked him to stay. The young doctor, last on the cricket field and first out of breath, had never before insisted on any desire. But suddenly, like a tide, he was unstoppable. He was going. He was going. His family, like his Heart, murmured in disapproval. He left his family behind. His disapproving Heart went with him.

His mother packed his suitcase with tea leaves, which came loose from their wrapping during the flight. When he went through customs, the agent opened the suitcase and asked him what it was. Tea—just tea that has come out of its package, sir, nothing to trouble you, Murali said. But Murali saw that the agent did not believe him. He felt himself beginning to sweat, and his Heart beginning to patter nervously. The agent called for a dog, and the dog came and smelled the suitcase and barked. Murali took his handkerchief out of his jacket pocket, knowing people were looking at him, this brown man with loose leaves in a suitcase. They had not even taken him to a private room. Embarrassing. The man called for his supervisor, who came and looked at Murali's passport again.

A doctor, eh? the supervisor said encouragingly, and Murali nodded mutely. What is this, doctor? He told you it was tea? The man lifted a handful of leaves to flared nostrils and inhaled. You idiot, you could have smelled it yourself—it *is* tea. Excellent tea, actually. Ceylon tea, probably. Let him through.

And the young doctor landed in America. He walked out into the cold. It was January, and New England, so it was cold. He had not known what that meant until this moment. As he looked out into the light and air of this place he discovered snow. The cold bit into his bones and he ignored it, because the snow was beautiful. But his Heart protested. *So cold here*, it murmured. Please do Shut Up, Murali told it politely. All his life he had been told his Heart was sick. He had seen his Heart himself; he was tired of its tiredness. What reason, after all, did it have to be tired? To hold him back? Fresh off the boat—so to speak, since it was actually a plane—he walked into the examining room of a heart specialist.

There is something wrong with my Heart, he said to the cardiologist.

Let's have a look, the American doctor said.

Another entrance into an X-ray machine, shirt unbuttoned to expose the Betraying Heart that had for so long offered the young doctor martyrdom. The lights flashed and the Eye of the machine entered his chest. Pumping, screaming, throbbing Heart. He closed his eyes. *So cold here*, the Heart murmured. *What are you doing here?* Shut *Up*, the young doctor told his body.

They pulled him out of the machine.

The cardiologist waited with him for the film to be developed. They talked in the meantime, kin, as all doctors are.

You're a resident?

Yes.

Where are you from?

A country where it is always warm, he said, and shivered.

Outside, it was still snowing. They looked at the film, pressed it against a viewer to read his innards, the maze of veins, the shape of his arteries. A glimpse into Eternity, an X-ray. Breathe in for me, the cardiologist said, pressing a chilly stethoscope to the skinny chest holding the Betraying Heart.

He put the stethoscope down.

There's nothing wrong with you, he said.

Thank you, said the young doctor, who was not yet my father, but edging ever closer.

VANI: HE MET HER, MY MOTHER, in New York City—which as always was full to the brim with immigrants—and the Heart said plaintively: *Thump thump thump.* That was not the sound of illness. Theirs was an auspicious meeting, although no one had troubled to check the alignment of the stars; the young woman was twenty-seven—old for a prospective bride?—but she did not look it. She had a generous face, he said to himself.

He liked her glossy sheaf of dark hair, her sparse brows, her pronounced chin, her full lower lip. She smiled with her mouth closed because she did not like her teeth. He could already see within the structure of her face how she would become thinner, that her bones would give her older face a certain elegance, a chiseled and austere severity. He liked her precision in even the smallest of tasks, like arranging hibiscus in a vase. Her reserve, her inability to say anything truly personal in public. He thought she might be full of secrets and wanted to know them. She never raised her voice, but she did not speak softly. *How are you? That's a beautiful sari. How are the children? I like this rice.* She liked her food steaming and spicy, as he did. She made her own clothes, staying up late into the night, her foot on the pedal of a Singer sewing machine that had belonged to her mother and had crossed the ocean with her. Her hemlines were high, and it suited both the times and her young pale slimness, which reminded him of a flowering tree by his home in Jaffna. He never caught her admitting she was wrong; her words clambered around that impossibility, but so sheepishly that he found it endearing. In a roomful of noisy Sri Lankans he learned to tell the clear bell sound of her bangles apart from the rest.

Suddenly, he was no longer thinking about widows or about repeating his own father's collapse. It was as though an invisible conductor was directing the pulling of strings to draw them together. Whether it was Murali who managed to get introduced to Vani or the other way around, no one else really remembers. And they will never admit which one of them was responsible. And yet, it was this simple: a friend of his noticed that they were staying near each other. Perhaps Murali could give Vani a ride home? Yes, yes, two heads nodded. They left the party they were at too quickly to say all their good-byes. After the door closed behind them the space where they had been was filled with the laughter of friends.

He took her home. She boarded with a family in Brooklyn. During the car ride they were silent. It was a strange and comfortable silence for two people who had waited for so long to be alone. The thrum of the motor was loud because the car was old. When they turned around the corner he pulled over and turned the engine off and there was a quiet as loud as the motor had been. He walked her to her door and she thanked him. She did not ask him in for a cup of coffee; it was not her house. But it was out of his way and both of them knew it. She forgot that she did not like her teeth and bared them at him. Her smile, for once, was not self-conscious. She watched him drive away, waving from the window. It is something Aravindrans always do for each other when they say good-bye.

THE SRI LANKAN ELDERS of New York City were all too eager to play parents to the couple. She was Proper: smart and polite and a good cook and lovely. Vani had a job, and more important than any of these things, she had grace, which was something that could not be taught. Murali, of course, was their Beloved Parentless Boy; their favorite bachelor-doctor whom they took into their homes and bosoms and tried to smother with welcome and curry. Friends can arrange a Marriage as easily as parents, they said among themselves, delighted. Occasions were arranged; even the very rooms seemed to conspire to make the two end up next to each other. And then one day something was suggested by one of those elders. And somehow the pair of them were *talking* about it. To each other. Directly.

Which was a faux pas. But neither of them minded.

OCEANS AWAY, FAMILIES EXPLODED. True to form, his family's discord faded quickly. But her family almost did not consent: afraid of the Improper, they questioned his intentions, his failure to observe certain formalities, his ancestry, his habits and character. He heard about what they had said and turned to her, his eyes full of questions.

They may not know these things about you, she said, but I do.

Are you sure? he asked her. The unsaid: they may not forgive you for this.

Positive, she answered. Countries away, Vani's brother, Kumaran, crashed into Murali's brother's house, yelling at the top of his lungs: *Who* is this doctor who wants to marry my *sister*? *Who* is this doctor who is *in love with my sister*?

The nerve of Murali, they thought. In Love? These were not words they were used to saying.

THE WEDDING: IT WAS CHEAP. Murali, growing closer to becoming my father, built the traditional wedding altar himself; he rented a local hall; he recruited the Sri Lankan elders to help with food and organization. Without the relatives who were scattered across the world, with the friends drawn close in New York City, the Marriage was Arranged.

There is a photograph of Vani looking very young and bashful and Proper in her Wedding-Red sari as he proposes a toast, her happiness veiled, her smile shy, so that no one could see it too clearly. *I never thought I would get married here,* her Heart said to his. *I never thought I could find you here.*

No one heard it, as is decent. Except—

Thump thump thump, replied the doctor's Heart, pleased at its success.

THIS IS NOT THE STORY they tell us at first. They say they did everything according to tradition, with methods of irreproachable propriety. And her family pretends they always loved him. But look again: Vani's brother Kumaran crashes through a door, yelling at the top of his lungs. When conflict begins depends, like everything else, on the memory you acquire or are given. But regardless of what Murali told her or did not tell her, conflict for Vani began with Kumaran, the sibling to whom she was closest and the one who sent my father a letter, telling him not to marry her. The one who emerged years later, bringing Vani's daughter a war and a country from which her mother had shielded her.

There is Proper Marriage; there is Improper Marriage.

EVEN NOW, MY PARENTS still love each other so much that they would never admit it. But no matter which version of the story you know or how softly you whisper it, Vani and Murali were married and became, at last, my parents. I told you a story about that place, and about their leaving it, but how do I know it? I am not the end of my parents' story, but I am the reason for its telling.

I am Yalini, their daughter. In July of 1983, I was born in the same New England that had welcomed my parents, Vani and Murali, into its arms so long ago. They had waited a long time for me. I came into the world squalling, as children should. As I was born, Murali held Vani's shoulders. I was born with jaundice. My hair was glossy like Vani's and wavy like Murali's. The nurses, gathered around my perspiring mother, said to each other that they had never seen a baby with quite that much hair. I came into a place anxious for my arrival. My parents, who did not know whether they should expect a daughter or a son, had already prepared a room for me. After Vani's water broke, Murali brought her into the hospital and announced that his child's room had already been painted pink. Now the nurse told him he would not have to redo it. It's a girl, the nurse said to Murali, at last my father. I was swaddled in blankets and placed in his arms. I immediately caught hold of his Heart with both tiny fists.

I was born in the early hours of the morning, on a day in late July. And as I entered this new world, my parents' old one was being destroyed.

BLACK JULY: MORE THAN two decades later, I think that almost every Sri Lankan Tamil knows what it means. I was born, and halfway around the world, Tamil people died, betrayed by their own country, which did nothing to save them.

Murali was in a hospital room with me and with Vani when a younger doctor came to get him.

Sir, there is—something. I think you will want to see it.

Murali moved to turn the television on in the room where we were sitting, but the other doctor looked at Vani and shook his head subtly: no.

Why don't you come with me, he said. Murali, sensing rising alarm in the other man, left us there and followed him down a long blue hospital hall, to a large waiting room, where the television was already on. My father's colleagues sat around it. They had been waiting for the new father to emerge, to offer him congratulations, to ask about baby weight and names. Now their good wishes died on their lips. No glad handshakes, no questions about the child. Instead they watched my father watching the news.

And there on the screen, my father saw everything he had once believed in, burning. Halfway around the world, in the country he had loved first and best, people were being killed for their Tamilness. The news showed anti-Tamil riots on the streets of Colombo, the capital of Sri Lanka, where members of the Sinhalese majority rioted against thousands of their Tamil countrymen. The news showed Tamil civilians beaten, robbed, and killed, their property seized and ruined. And the Sri Lankan government had done nothing to defend them. My father watched, and saw that he had constructed his life inside laws that were nothing more than a house of cards.

Standing there, Murali thought of his classmates, his friends, his old village neighbors, some of whom were almost certainly in Colombo. Later, he would hear stories of organized mobs stopping vehicles on the streets, looking for Tamils. He would hear that those they had discovered were stabbed or set aflame. Later, he would come to understand that government authorities had handed enraged rioters voter lists, which showed ethnicity, so that they could go door-to-door and hunt down their Tamil neighbors, coworkers, and schoolmates. He would read about the government's failure to declare and enforce curfews. Later, people would debate emigration, asylum, property damage, and casualty numbers. Later, he would mourn, when he learned which of his friends had been among those attacked.

And later, Tamil separatist groups would rise, newly powerful, from the ashes of those riots—their ranks strengthened by the young people whose families had been hurt in 1983 and before. Those young people would have no reason to believe in Sri Lanka, and so they would become militants. Rebels who would fight for a separate nation for Sri Lankan Tamils in the decades to come. Of these, one group would emerge the strongest: the Liberation Tigers of Tamil Eelam. They would blow themselves up to take others with them, targeting symbols and representatives of the state; they would attack civilians and eat cyanide to avoid imprisonment. They would kill other Tamils who did not agree with them—other rebels, politicians, and even civilians. They would fight against a government that shelled, starved, and tortured its own citizens. They would renounce their families and bring children and women into their ranks.

They would be called terrorists. They would enter into a world in which no one was right.

Murali did not know any of that yet. But standing there at that moment, he knew that he had left Sri Lanka totally and absolutely. He would not retire there, or grow old there, or die there. He would go back, perhaps after a long time, for a visit of a month or perhaps two. But he could never live there again. And he had never really believed that before.

He was a father now. Murali looked around the room at the doctors who worked with him and realized how alone he was in this roomful of friends. Their faces were full of sympathy, but they did not understand who he was. They never would.

MY PARENTS NAMED ME YALINI, after the part of their home that they loved the most. It is a Tamil name, with a Tamil home: a name that means, in part, *Jaffna, Sri Lanka,* the place from which they came. In Sri Lanka children do not leave their parents or resist becoming them. They fall into it easily, gracefully, take their mantles of responsibility without protest. Even those who became rebels have inherited their parents' struggles from the days after independence, and before 1983.

But I grew up and out of my parents' house. I grew up and went to a university far away from them. At this school my work consumed me, because that was what I wanted. I mired myself in it. I called my parents infrequently, in the snatches of time between work and class, or class and meals, or lying down and sleeping. I grew up, went to school, and went away from my parents. I left their war-torn house in our peaceful country.

There, Away, I became more like them than ever before, because no matter how American I was, I was also the only Sri Lankan. I was alone as my mother had been, stepping onto her first escalator in New York. As alone as my father had been inside the X-ray machine, before meeting my mother.

EVERYTHING IN THIS PLACE—so far from the home my parents had constructed for me—felt old and unremarkable. I had made myself unable to be surprised, and so I took no joy in my first independence, as my parents had taken in theirs. I had traveled a great distance, and my eyes were tired and saw nothing fresh. If you had found me there then and asked me what I missed, I could not have given you an answer.

At the university, the other students only made me feel lonelier. I went there in the fall of 2001, and two weeks after I left my parents, terrorists attacked their adopted country, the country in which I had been born, and that I loved. Everything around us fell into disaster, in a place where we had thought that impossible. War had always mattered to me, and now, finally, far too late, it mattered to everyone else too. When I finally went to the airport to go home again on the first holiday, the faces of the security men made me think of my father and his loose tea leaves, the story he had told me of the dog barking at him so many years earlier. Their faces searched mine, or I imagined that they did. I thought of my father as a very young and innocent man and felt a strange cold gladness in being a woman, as though it made me safer, although in fact all it did was make my life more dangerous in different ways.

When I stepped off the plane, I gripped my father's shoulders and kissed him. He seemed smaller to me. I seemed smaller to myself.

SCHOOL DID NOT MAKE me happy, but that had nothing to do with the school itself, and everything to do with me. And of course I went back there. Perhaps I thought that as a Sri Lankan, it was my obligation to reenter my own misery without naming it. If it had not been for the obvious despair of the world around me, I would have seen my own unhappiness earlier.

In the cold, dim weeks after what happened, the world looked at once more dangerous and more welcoming. The weather seemed cold, although it was not yet winter. The ground was still green, but it became harder and colder, as though readying itself for snow. People who would never have stopped to speak to each other before met each other's eyes squarely with what they thought was honesty. I thought that this was a lie; this was temporary. People did not care about each other like this. I felt certain that people would return to the way they had been before, as though nothing had happened. Students who lived with me gathered to talk about what had happened, but I did not join them, because that would have accomplished nothing. I wanted to be alone. I wanted to read. I went to the library and studied, even when our professors canceled their lectures and classes.

In the library, I liked to read at a particular long, dark table. My father had taught me to treasure libraries. He had done this by repeating the story of his own childhood library, the Jaffna Public Library, which had been burned by thugs in 1981, two years before I was born, as members of the Sri Lankan cabinet looked on and did nothing. I looked around this American university library and noted its fire alarms and fire extinguishers. Security personnel stood at each entrance. This library was well guarded, if not well loved. In Jaffna, many irreplaceable single-copy manuscripts had burned. As a child, I had imagined it many times, in each library I had entered—men in uniforms laughing, with torches and gasoline and guns. How each shelf would fall into and break the one below it, wood blackening and metal melting. How the cover of one book would embrace the one beside it, touching it gently, so gently, with a ring of sparks.

Nothing would burn here. In fact, during these days it was almost empty. Nobody else ever sat there, because the chairs lining the table were uncomfortable. I preferred these chairs because they made it difficult to sleep and easy to focus. Every day, after breakfast, before class, I went to that table in the library. Light came in from a long, low window above it, and the books on the shelves around it stood dusty and undisturbed. No one came there because the books were about histories that had ceased being interesting to anybody. Sometimes, if I was very tired, I laid my head down against the edge of the table to rest. After a few minutes, the sharp edge would wake me up again. If you had asked me what I was studying there, I could not have told you.

One morning, I had laid my head down on the edge of the table to close my eyes for a moment when someone tapped me on the shoulder. A tall, pale boy held a book out to me. His hair, so brown it was almost black, needed to be cut. His finely drawn, open face looked younger than mine.

I found this in the library yesterday, he said. I think it has your name in it. Aren't you Yalini?

I blinked at him. He stood slightly taller than my father, perhaps six feet. He had a firm but generous mouth. I took the book from him without touching his hand. It was a leather journal of the kind found in large bookstores. My father had given it to me for my last birthday. A strap wound around it held it closed. Without thinking, I unwound the strap and flipped through its pages. This revealed nothing because I had never written in it. I had left it in the library without missing it because it had not yet become important to me to write things down.

It's blank, he said.

Thank you, I said. I hadn't realized that I had left something here.

I didn't open it, he said. I saw you get up without it.

He looked at me, and I thought that he was going to leave, but he stood there. I turned back toward the table so that my shoulders were set against him. I had finished talking to him. But he did not leave. He came around to the other side of the table and sat down as though we were going to continue the conversation.

I had never before met a person who had decided to be my friend without waiting for my consent.

HE HAD DECIDED THAT we were friends. In that long, blank time when everyone treated everyone else with a false equivalence, that meant something to me, and I did not want to argue with the generosity of his persistence. We were friends for three years. Then, in the winter of 2004, I went home to spend the holidays with my parents.

On the day after Christmas, I was walking out the door with my mother when someone called: my mother's sister, Kalyani. My mother turned around to pick up the phone.

Ah, my mother said. All right. We will call back.

She hung up.

What did she say? I asked.

Something about water in Sri Lanka, my mother said. Something bad happening. Let's go.

Something bad was always happening. Later, I thought how tired she must have been, how weary of the updates from the front. For years she had taught herself to avoid them. Or maybe it was just that her sister, in trying to be gentle, had not told her enough to make her understand. None of us had used the word *tsunami* yet. No one understood what it meant.

We walked out the door and into the winter sun.

BY THE TIME THE CAR rounded the first corner away from the house, my relatives in Australia had called my relatives in Germany, who called my relatives in France, who called my relatives in England and Canada. They called us again. The phone rang and the house was empty. Watch the news, they said into the recording. The earth had shifted, and in doing so, moved the ocean. Water rolled over Sri Lankan homes, over fields, over trees, over temples, into the sky.

IN THE DAYS AFTER THAT, when my phone rang, I did not pick it up. It seemed like that first fall, three years earlier. I did not want to pick up the phone and hear concern that I knew would disappear. My friend called my phone, and I did not answer. He called the house, and when my mother gave me the message, I shook my head: no. I could not stand the idea of that in his voice. I watched the news and saw bodies. We did not know if anyone in our family had died, and then we learned that someone related to me had gone to the temple and drowned there, in a place full of water and gods. I had never met him and felt no right to any grief. I sat tearless before the news. And the news talked about the war, our war, as though it had just begun again. Dear Americans, there has been a war in this place. As though there had been no war for the decades before this. I heard my father say, bitterly, that at least now people would be able to find Sri Lanka on a map.

I have never been one for talking, and I did not want to talk to my friend, because he seemed too far outside this. He seemed too far away from everything I missed. He came from a place full of people who were just learning about war, and I realized then that I had grown up full of it, without realizing it, and that I did not know what to say about it to anyone, even my parents, who were still the people I loved the most. I had been born lucky, outside of war and unable to forget it. We came from different worlds, my friend and I, even though we had both grown up in America, in houses that in my parents' country would be considered rich. There was still a space there. It would have taken bravery to walk across that divide, and at that moment, water in my head, I did not have it. I was sorry for the difference between us and too tired to reach through it. Without waiting for my consent, he had decided that we would be friends; now, without waiting for his consent, I cut him off.

I cut him off and then I did not think of him. I thought of those bodies in the water, and even more, the bodies before them.

I WANTED, FINALLY, to be a doctor. My father had used medicine as a way out of Sri Lanka. I wanted it as a way in. But that was not possible. I went to my father and said *I want to go* and he looked at me and said,

Are you trying to kill me?

I don't want to go back to school, I said. Not now.

Bodies in their many shapes have always fascinated me—their infinite variety and similarity, the perfect machinery of each limb and sinew. But this was different. I wanted to go to a hospital, to pick up children who looked like me. I had pushed my American friends away, thinking their concern false, but I was just as guilty. It should not have taken this to make me want medicine. The reasons had been there all along. The irony, of course, is that natural disaster had made Sri Lanka relatively safe for the first time. At least temporarily. Even so, that was not what my father wanted for me. It was more than he could bear, that idea. He did not believe that even God in his anger could have opened up such a window of peace. He did not need to tell me that he thought it would not last. He said it like this:

You can come to work with me.

My father's patients were children with cancer, some of them with radiation-stripped heads so small I could cup them in the palm of one hand. But I entered into the hospital with war still in my head, and I did not really see them. I knew what my friend would have said, even though I did not regret not picking up the phone. He would have known, watching me, that I was not really there. For a whole year, inside my head, I was swimming somewhere else, in the low, dull, swelling current of another storm. Even on that small planet of dying children, I felt nothing but the effort of keeping my head above water.

ALTHOUGH I WOULD HAVE said otherwise once, my mother was not to blame for this. My mother, Vani, was born with grace, but I had to learn it, so I learned it from her. My mother will not show fear, because then it counts; she will not betray anger, knowing how it could come back to hurt her later; she will put your needs before hers without ever letting you know she has done this, because her mother did this, and her mother before her, and her mother too before that. I wanted that mask for myself because I realized for the first time how unprotected I felt in the world. Although my father had once been caught by what he considered the transparency of her face, its pure, clear quality, to me her expression is most remarkable for its ability to give away nothing.

And like that, her voice gave away nothing when she called me in August of 2005. It was the week before school started again, and at last I had left my father's hospital and gone back to campus to finish my degree, as I had promised him I would. I stood in my room, surrounded by suitcases and boxes and books. The phone, covered with dust, rang and I reached to pick it up.

Buy a plane ticket, my mother said, and meet us in Toronto.

She never asks for anything, but for some reason I was not surprised at this, or at my *yes* traveling across the phone line, through a wire, over the many miles that parted us. She guards her expression, but to think that she feels nothing—that would be a mistake. That was not a lesson she had taught me. I had learned to feel nothing on my own.

IT USED TO BE that you could be anyone and no one at the airport. My parents came to this country through airports. Who needs the romance of ships? This is nothing compared to propellers, to wings, the long sweet lay of the land down below you. The plane, touching down, enters a new, borderless place. In the terminals of the great cities of the world, we hold passports, but not countries. We move freely with one another. We pay taxes to no one. We arrive; we depart. We collect the detritus of our lives from baggage carrousels. We anticipate great pleasure and pain, comings and goings. This is true even now, as countries have begun to guard their borders more closely, against the fear of enemies and bombs, against the fear of people who look like my father, my brother, my uncle, and my cousins. People live more vividly in airports.

My mother had asked me to meet her in an airport. She had told me which ticket to buy, which hour to arrive, what clothes to pack. I stood by the baggage carrousel in the wide, gray space of arrivals and waited where she had told me to wait. I stood on first one foot and then the other, picking each leg up carefully and setting it down in turn, my impatience barely in check. I believed in traveling light, and had no bags to collect. The carrousel went around to my right, and then a girl moved into my view from the left.

She was unexpected and lovely, because she looked like me, but also not like me. She stood taller, and looked fairer, by which I mean her skin in the harsh light of that space seemed lighter than mine. She was about my age. Her even, regular features looked like my mother's—the sparse eyebrows, the full lower lip, the sharp chin. She had closed her mouth against smiling without looking precisely unhappy. My father had once looked at my mother and seen the face she would later own. This girl's face was like my mother's, but she had no later face inside it. As though she did not believe that there would be a later.

JANANI: SHE WAS MY COUSIN, although I did not know that yet. She looked like my mother, and like her father, although I did not know that yet either. I saw her before I saw her father, because he was in a wheelchair, and although he was still tall, in his sitting position his eyes did not naturally meet mine. He saw me before I saw him and recognized me. Later, he told me that he was already sorry in that first moment for what he had done decades before. In seeing me, he understood for the first time that what he had done could have led to my not standing there.

Janani moved into my view, pushing him in the wheelchair. Although I did not yet see him, he saw me and began to understand something: he would want to give me an explanation.

I chose to know this story, all its sides and wonders. But first someone came to me and offered to tell it.

WHEN I SAW HIM my mouth fell open slightly, my surprise tumbling out of it finally, if in silence. Restrained a little. After all, I am my mother's daughter too.

He murmured something upward to Janani, and she stopped the wheelchair perhaps five steps away from me. She turned toward me, following the direction of his thin, pale finger to meet my eyes.

You must be Yalini, she said in Tamil. I do not speak Tamil, but I understand it, and I understood her. Still, I did not have time to speak before he did something even more astonishing: he stood up and stepped forward, out of the wheelchair. I made a sound as if to stop him, but I was too slow. He walked the five steps between us very slowly, and I did not understand why Janani did not intervene. His shoulders loomed broadly, but they trembled. He looked as though he might fall down at any moment, but then, finally, he stood before me, taller than me, taller than my father. Unlike her, he had kept some strength in reserve. He had been saving something all this time, all this time he had been gone. Saving it for me, although he had just now realized it.

KUMARAN: MY UNCLE. HE was done with crashing through doors and writing letters. He was done with war, although I did not know that yet. It was him, of course. That I knew, although he had been gone for so long that we had never met.

He stood very tall, and his pale scalp shone through the too-fine threads of his hair, the thinning hair not of someone old, but of someone sick. He looked mortally tired, blue-veined under deep-set eyes, but he had a finely cut face too, a look that belonged in my mother's family. He shook a little, standing, and I reached out automatically to steady him. His wrist was bone-dry, his skin like parchment. His eyes, with the coldness of mountains, beginning to warm. His mouth starting to scab where his lips had cracked in the dry air of the flight. He stood as straight as he could, which was not very straight, but I could see the stance he aimed for, a posture I would later describe not as militant but as military. Despite the effort, he leaned slightly, favoring one side, as though some part of him had been damaged and had healed improperly. It had, but that too, I did not know until later. His hairline shone wetly with the work of standing there. I saw that, and finally I understood where he must have been all these years and why I had never met him. In a moment I filled up with my own past and saw that I had always known where he was. I had always known that he was a Tamil Tiger, although no one had ever told me. Nor had anyone told me why he was here now, but still I knew it: he was here to die. Not in a fight, or for a cause, but at the whim of nature. Because it was time.

His daughter had brought the wheelchair behind him without a sound, and without looking, without reaching a hand out to make sure that it was there, he lowered himself into it. I stood there, my hand still on his wrist, uncertain. And then my parents were there. I did not see them coming. Later, when I knew what had happened between all of them, when I knew that cancer was growing inside him, I went back to that picture in my mind: my mother and, behind her, my father. I tried to recollect the shape of my father's mouth. Did he crush the anger out of it? Did my mother, with her careful, quiet eye, see him do it? Or was it too late for anger? Are you forgiven everything if you are dying?

I do remember that my father looked very dark to me, as though I were seeing him with someone else's eyes. He pushed an empty luggage trolley. My mother, already ahead of him, bent to embrace her brother—even in her tears anticipating both his desire to stand and his inability to do it again. She wept nakedly and I almost did too, out of fear rather than real sadness. Empathy welled up inside me like a foreign creature. I had never seen my mother cry before. Later, my father told me that before I was born, he took my mother to England, to meet her mother, after they had been apart for years. When he opened the door to that house, he said, my mother wept like that, as though she remembered everything for the first time.

Now, as then, he did not know what to do with her tears. He looked at the trolley, and at Janani.

We haven't brought anything, she said.

Nothing, my father said. Then, again, as though this was too incredible: Nothing?

Nothing, she said.

Even the wheelchair, which my uncle needed but did not want, belonged to someone else. We left it at the airport and moved slowly beyond its perimeter, toward a new life.

KUMARAN: HE CAME TO us bearing nothing, truly—except certain implied conditions. He had been one of the Tigers, once, and they had let him go, although they were famous for never letting anyone go. He had spent his life as a rebel, but now he was dying, and he had a daughter. The Tigers had once said: join us, and we are your family. Leave the *ūr*, your place of origin, in order to fight for it. They were his family, and then they were not. They let him go and, in doing so, made him promise not only his loyalty, but also ours. They let him go only in body. He did not say this to my parents. But my father said it to me. I think he wanted to make sure that I understood what my uncle's presence cost them.

My father thought that price was worth it, because of how much he loved my mother, and how much my mother loved her brother. My mother had never really spoken of him. I had never even seen a picture. In my parents' house the only pictures of children were pictures of me. In the 1983 riots, fire in her sister's Colombo house had consumed the early pictures of my mother and her family; those remaining showed her in New York, wearing those dresses she had made on the Singer sewing machine. The pictures of my father as a child had never existed.

But I must have known about my uncle nevertheless. As a child I cherished a habit of listening at doors. And although my mother had never spoken of him, my father had, if only to tell me that my mother had a brother who had disappeared.

I was perhaps twelve. I stood in the doorway of my father's study. Be careful with your mother today, he said.

What? Why?

Don't ask questions, he said and then sighed. It's her brother's birthday.

Her brother?

Your uncle, Kumaran, my father said. He disappeared a long

time ago. Back There. He waved a hand vaguely, as though he did not know the direction he meant. We both knew the direction he meant.

Is he dead? I asked, not yet old enough not to ask that question.

No, my father said.

I was old enough not to ask where he was. Where else could he have been? If my mother walked into a room and saw me watching the news, she turned away. I knew about the war and could guess at what it had taken from my parents. But I had never thought it could take anything away from me.

In a car heading away from the airport and into Toronto, I finally became old enough not to ask questions. If I had been younger, I might have asked: Where are we going? If you are one of them, how did you get here? How do you have a daughter? The Tigers are famous for their discipline—their dedication to a single cause: the Tamil homeland. Tigers don't have families.

But they do. They do. They live, they marry, they bear children, and they die. Saying they do not cannot erase this. The bearing of arms cannot erase this.

KUMARAN: WITH HIM, now we too were trapped. We could not take him back into the United States. He would be arrested as an illegal, and certainly also for his past affiliation with the Tigers, whom some nations, including mine, call terrorists. But Toronto is different. He had come to Canada, having passed through London with forged papers, and now that he was here, we knew that he would not be sent back. Canada's arms had always been more open. After what had happened in 1983, many Sri Lankan Tamils had come here for asylum and refuge. Now, in 2005, the Canadian immigration authorities had flagged him. Caught. For someone else, it might have been over. But at their prompting, he had produced the Sri Lankan national ID card with his real name. He said *Tiger.* I can imagine how the knowledge of his history spread across their faces with something that was not quite alarm. *We know this man has done things that would make his mother weep.* But his mother had already done her weeping.

He also carried a letter, signed by a Sri Lankan physician, which promised a definite terminus to his stay. *This man is dying.* Cancer of the brain. He said *refugee,* he said *Tiger,* and they saw how sick he was. Too sick to send back. My father too, vouched for this. They said *Yes. You may die here.* My father handed over his passport and signed a paper that claimed responsibility for my uncle. I did not know then what that meant. I love my father, because in the end, he was everyone's doctor. Anyone he could help.

TORONTO: FOR YEARS, Tamil refugees of my parents' country had found their way here, stumbling toward the blooming garden of Little Jaffnas, a space that, while it is not home, has the redeeming quality of being arranged in the same way. A place where a newly transplanted blind man might walk into the grocery store and know instinctively where to find the cashews, the bread, the mangoes. This Toronto insisted on its very Tamilness in a way that was both comforting and dangerous. America had never offered me anything like this. On my birthday, the anniversary of Black July, the Tamils of Canada gathered in open assemblies to praise their new country for saving them. Later, Canada too would say the Tigers were terrorists, but then, when my uncle entered the country, they had not yet been named anything forbidden.

My father called another Tamil physician, who met us at St. Anthony's Hospital. We were admitted with no questions, and my uncle was placed on a gurney and wheeled away. An intravenous line already threaded into his arm, his wrist, where I had held it. They wanted to rehydrate him because he had been vomiting on the plane. My cousin did not try to go with him. She watched impassively. Her father resisted nothing about the sterile implements of sedation around him.

When he was gone, my mother asked her if she had eaten anything. No, she had not. My father pressed some money into my hand for the hospital cafeteria: go and buy some food, he said.

We walked to the elevator together, she and I. It was the first time we had walked anywhere together. The elevator seemed very small, and we did not speak to each other. I leaned against the metal rail at the back, and she looked at me, or rather my mirrored reflection, in the mirrored walls. She wore a linen blouse of the type that my mother sometimes wore, the buttons too big and far apart, the collar conservatively cut and high, the sleeves too big for her skinny, strongly muscled arms. Her bearing too, was slightly military. I knew stories about the Tigers and children, about the Tigers and women who had taught her to carry herself like that. She kept her hands folded in front of her, and her slender, neat braid neared her waist. Her long skirt almost touched the floor. Her sandals looked new, but that did not matter: it was already fall, and we would need to get rid of them before winter came. I remembered my mother telling me that she had never worn a covered shoe before coming to the United States.

Janani did not follow me but rather walked alongside me as we went down another long, blue hospital corridor, her eyes darting around, assessing everything carefully. She was not nervous, but her eyes were watchful. Although I had never seen the darkness of the Jaffna Teaching Hospital and could not have imagined its bullet-pocked walls, I thought that she must never have seen anything like that hospital cafeteria before. She did not look disoriented or confused. I pointed her toward the tea, found two plates, and heaped them with overcooked white rice and curries. The hospital did have curries—probably because of all the Tamil doctors and patients here. This will be like home for her, I thought—rice and tea. Dark curry, brown faces.

I paid for the food and then we sat down. I pushed a plate toward her, across the wooden table, which was not made of real wood. She handed me a cup of tea, waiting until she was sure I was holding it to let go. Later, I realized that this must have all seemed very inhospitable to her, very Improper. As a girl raised in Jaffna, she would have known that a host does not eat with a guest. I had never been taught that. Which one of us was the host here? I thought it might be me and felt inadequate. She was a conservative girl, a Proper girl. Not as Proper as I thought—she had traded her father's plot of Jaffna land to a man, to another man, to another man, in exchange for aid with her father's journey. But she told me none of that. She claimed none of the escape for herself. She drank her tea and looked at me, unsmiling.

Your mother and father didn't say anything, she said. They didn't tell you we were coming. This time she spoke in English, and I could tell that her mouth was out of practice. Her e's sounded like a's, and her a's tilted upward into i's.

No, I said. How old are you?

She frowned, trying to remember the number in English. Finally she said it in Tamil. I nodded my understanding.

Eighteen. She was four years younger than me. Later, I would do the math of it and see how it had worked: in 1984, the year after I was born, the leader of the Tamil Tigers, who had once proscribed marriage for his cadres, had fallen in Love. Like anyone else. And within a few years, that love had made other love possible, and here was my cousin, sitting before me, looking like me and not like me.

Now I asked:

Where is your mother? In English.

My mother was in the movement too, she said. She was killed a few years ago in a bombing. She said the whole sentence in Tamil except for *bombing*. She did not pause between the first and second sentences, and that made it easier for me to move past my regret at asking the question. I still wanted to know: What kind of bombing? Was she the bomber or the bombed?

I did not ask, because although Janani's still face was not a locked gate, neither was it an invitation. She did not look at all sad. She tipped the sugar canister into her tea, and far too much sugar came out of it. She stirred and drank as though she did not believe that too much of anything could have a consequence.

They just let you come with your father? I asked.

She stopped sipping and I saw her decide to slow down so that I would understand her.

In slower Tamil: I wanted to come with my father, she said,

but also, I did not want to leave. That was my home, you know? She studied my face. No, you have never been there, she said. I can already see that you do not know anything about it.

The war? I know about the war.

You barely understand me, she said. How could you know about the war? You grew up without speaking Tamil? The war is like Tamil for you. Something you would learn about only if you had to, not because you chose to. We have heard about Tamils abroad. The convenience of their belief.

I must have turned red. She was Proper, but still direct. You could be Proper and angry, I saw.

I speak Tamil, I said. A little.

Go ahead and speak it then, she said. You are an American. Not very Tamil, I think, or you would already be married. But I will be married before you.

You are going to be married? I asked.

I am here to be with my father when he dies, she said. He is going to die. I know that. I would have preferred that he die there, in the place that he, we, fought for. That we wanted. The place where I grew up, where my real family is. Where my mother died.

Her face twisted a little at that.

I wanted that for him, she said, but he wanted to be here with your mother. I think she must have been his favorite sister, even despite the way that she got married.

We had already sat for hours in waiting lounges, in airport offices and hospitals, to get my uncle to this place. My father had confirmed for me who my uncle was. And he had told me, in not so many words, that certain people would expect things of us because Kumaran was here now. But neither my mother nor my father had mentioned anything about Janani marrying.

They did not tell you about that either, she said. And then, in a different voice: I suppose it's possible that my father has not told them yet.

She waited for me to say something, but I did not.

There is a man who lives here, in Toronto, she said. His name is Vijendran. He does a lot of work for Eelam. That is the name of our country, the homeland we were fighting for. Do you even know that? And this man has a son. He is my intended.

You're *eighteen*, I said.

Old enough, she said. Our grandmother was married with children at that age. My mother is dead and my father will be dead and then I will have no one.

What about us? I asked.

She looked at me.

Your parents are kind, she said. But they are not my family. You are not my family.

She did not know yet that that was not her choice to make. We would each try and fail at this: to leave our families behind.

NOW, FINALLY, A YEAR later and years too late, death has done what no one else could do, not even Kumaran himself: it has made him no longer a militant, no longer a Tamil Tiger. He is no longer here. And his daughter is the one about to be Properly Married.

Later that week, we took him from the hospital. He had told my father, not my mother, that he did not want to die in a hospital. And so arrangements had been made—by whom or how, I did not ask. We went to an empty house on the edge of Scarborough, a particularly Tamil part of Toronto. We put my uncle in a hospital bed and scheduled regular visits from a hospital nurse. We put my uncle in a bed to die, surrounded by us.

Watching my mother I could tell that she was glad to do it, that to care for my uncle as he died made her happier than she had been, not knowing where he was. She would rather he died in her presence than lived his previous life. She did not want to imagine him in other places. She changed his sheets, made his favorite curries, read to him, and played the Tamil music he loved in his room. In the morning she drew his curtains, and in the evening, she closed them. Sometimes Janani helped her, but mostly she just seemed to wait, and wait. For what, I did not know. She sat on the sill of the window facing the backyard and watched everything. The window faced an English-style garden, a small patch of gray ground, with a waist-high fence and trellis peeling white paint and dead leaves and branches. The whole world bloomed around that garden, but it did not grow a thing. Although it was naked of any life, if my uncle had the energy my mother and he sometimes walked, very slowly, arm in arm around that garden, so that he could get some fresh air.

During the days my father generally left them alone. But he rose before my mother, and in the very early, cold dawn, when only he and my uncle were awake, he would go into my uncle's room and do the daily checkup. Once, I woke up too, sweating, and, on the way to get a glass of water, heard them.

Breathe in, my father said. Then: How's the pain?

My uncle muttered something I could not hear, his Tamil too fast for me to understand.

I can give you some pills, my father said. It will be similar to morphine.

Cyanide, my uncle said. He laughed roughly, but genuinely, and I felt a sudden rush of liking. I leaned back against the cool white wall. It was still dark. My father had not turned any lights on. But he must have heard me moving, because he came out into the hall and saw me standing there.

Go back to bed, he said gently.

I did not move.

Well, if you are not going, he said then, very slowly and hesitantly, you could go and talk to your uncle.

THE LIGHTS WERE NOT on in that room, but the dull light of the morning came in through the windows, and the hospital bed was white, so I could see his face clearly. He had raised the bed halfway, and a book, a familiar copy of the *Tirukkural* that I thought might belong to my father, lay open on his chest. He looked so strange to me. His face was my mother's, but it was a dying face. And so I had not really wanted to see him. Mostly he had been in pain, and that kind of pain felt new to me, even watching it from the outside. No one I had truly known had ever died, and I did not want to truly know him. In that abandoned house, which was abandoned even as we lived in it, we did not know each other. I had not talked to him. I rose, I read, I helped my mother, and I slept.

I was wondering if you were ever going to come and talk to me, he said in Tamil. He patted the bed next to his knee. Sit and tell me about yourself.

I did not sit down. What do you want to know? in English.

What are you studying? Still in Tamil.

English, I said.

He laughed. Well, that explains it. What are you going to do?

I'm going to be a doctor, I told him, and that made it real, suddenly.

Do you speak Tamil?

I understand it.

Are all the children here like that?

Well, we're not like your daughter, I said before I could stop myself.

He laughed again, harder this time. Then his face jerked suddenly, and again I saw that enormous physical pain bearing down on him. I felt sick, but he made his face stay in the smile. I admired that almost against my will.

I do not think that anyone is like my daughter. I know that

you have not talked about it with your father, but he knows, and your mother knows. It is true, that she is going to be Married. That is what she wants. It is her way of supporting the world she and I have left.

She can do whatever she wants, I said.

I wanted to tell you something, he said. In English now. A story. But you want to leave. It would be easier to leave, that's true.

Something in me rose up at the tone in his voice, although I knew he was baiting me.

I didn't say that I wanted to leave, I said.

You don't know me, he said. You didn't have to say that you wanted to leave. Why would you want to know me, when I have caused your mother such grief? Perhaps I will only cause you grief. How old are you? I'd like you to stay. I can manage the English, if you want. Once, long ago, I spoke only English. The Queen's English, actually. You should be in school, no? How much time do you have?

I think the question is how much time do *you* have? I said.

Long enough, he said.

KUMARAN: HE SAID, I want to tell you that your father is an exceptional man. Do you see that your father is taking care of me, even after what I did to him? I wrote to him, you know, and not to your mother, because I thought that it would be too hard for her. I wanted to spare her the arrangements, the logistics of bringing me here. Your father did too. He has always wanted to spare her any grief.

We are not friends, my uncle said. We have never been friends. But your father is an exceptional man.

I sat still for a moment. After what you did to him? I asked.

Ah, my uncle said. He is even more exceptional than I thought. He did not tell you. He left it for me. I deserve to have to tell you. When your father wanted to marry your mother, I tried to stop him. You know where I was, don't you? Do children here know about the war?

We know about the war, I said. As a child, we used to receive newsletters about it. Unofficial publications, because no one would publish anything official. I remember that the newsletter used to come, and if I got home before my father, I could manage to read it.

What did you read?

It was very graphic, I said and shuddered. I had been very young. Much of the information had been in Tamil, but I remembered the bits in English. I had been an early reader. My father had come home from work one day and found me reading descriptions of torture. In the rough English of the nonnative speaker, the writer had detailed scenes inside army facilities: Tamil men hung upside down, the soles of their feet burned, their private parts laid bare to fire ants and electrocution. Answer the question, those men were told: Are you a Tiger?

I was a Tiger, my uncle said. I am a Tiger.

I thought that once you joined the Tigers, you couldn't leave, I said.

They couldn't use me like this, he said. I became sick and there was nothing they could do about it. Perhaps they think I can be more useful here. People here have money. They, we, are very intelligent. I'm sure you know. We became famous. We bombed the airport and killed no one. We even drove the Indian forces out of Sri Lanka. We were very clever. We did all this with nothing. We had nothing compared to the armies of Sri Lanka, the armies of India. I was with them from almost the beginning, and I was with them for a long time. They made it possible for me to leave. People talk about their rules, but no one knows about their exceptions. Nothing there is hard and fast. How can war be hard and fast? It's a very long war. It changes. It evolves. War does.

Like the rule against Marriage, I said.

He blinked, surprised that I knew that much. Yes, he said. When the Tigers began, when the boys began to form the movement, one of the ideas was that we had to be disciplined, and that that kind of love was a distraction from our goals. We were just coming to arms, after a long time of trying peaceful methods. In the 1970s, people everywhere were becoming radicals, even in America. And I was just coming to arms. I was young. I should have been at university. That was what had happened to a lot of us—we should have been at university, and because of what had happened to Tamils who wanted to study, we felt there was nothing else we could do. What else could we do? I had been gone already, gone awhile, when I heard through some rumors that your father wanted to marry your mother. For me, the university was a place where the political world was born. I began to believe in things there, things and people other than God, when before I had only believed in the ties of blood. For your father, the university was a way out, a way to a place where he met your mother. I do not even remember how I heard about the two of them. I was so angry about everything, and especially about that. My sister in another world outside mine. Your mother had exited the place where we grew up, and your father meant that that exit would be permanent. She was supposed to come back to Sri Lanka. I wanted her to come back. I wanted to think that we all had a future there.

What did you do? I asked.

No one cares about a small country, he said. People will tell you otherwise, but it's true. The country of your parents is not important in your country, or even in this half of the world. I was angry for that reason. You don't seem angry about anything. That's very unusual in a young person.

I'm angry, I said. For the first time in many months, that was true.

I mean anger about a political situation. Look at my daughter, your cousin, Janani. She's angry at me for leaving Sri Lanka, for leaving the Tigers. For bringing her to this country, when we fought so hard for that one. Her mother died there and she wants to think that it was for a good reason. The Tigers are the only thing she has known. Life inside the country they are making, with so much work. She sees you and she thinks that you are privileged. She thinks your life is easy. Is she wrong? What are you angry about? I was a young person, and I wanted certain traditions to be maintained. We came from a good family, and I am your mother's older brother. Vani's marriage was part of my responsibility. I wrote a letter to your father.

What did the letter say? I asked.

In the letter I wrote many things that I could never take back, he said. I wish I could take them back. I wrote to your father and I told him that I was part of the movement, that I could find his family. Hurt them.

I leaned forward and looked at my uncle, hard. He stared back, unblinking, the whites of his eyes veined with red, his hands shaking. I could tell that once his mouth had looked like my mother's, but now his lips pressed together, thin and uncompromising.

You threatened my father's family? I said.

I didn't stop him from doing what he wanted, my uncle said. I don't know whether he believed me or not, what he thought I could do. Your father wanted to marry your mother.

This is the story you wanted to tell me, I said in disbelief.

I thought someone should tell you, he said. I think I was jealous of your father before, but I was never more jealous of him than I was at the airport, when I saw you standing next to Janani. Look at how different you are, the things you inherited. I don't know if I meant it, but that was what I wrote.

Is that the whole story? I asked him.

Of course not, he said. But what else are we doing here? I can tell you the whole story.

No, you can't, I said. Part of it is my father's.

MY FATHER GOT A leave of absence from the university hospital where he worked and taught, and my mother, the teacher, found a temporary replacement. And I called my university and told them that once again, I was not returning. I was surprised that my parents did not reprimand me. They had left Sri Lanka, after all, so that I—not yet their daughter—could have an education. I did not know my uncle, not really, and so my mother, at least, had not actually expected me to stay. It's possible that my father did, but after all, he had received that first letter from my uncle so many years before, and he had also been the one to receive the letter saying that my uncle was coming to Canada. My father might not have been surprised that I stayed. He was surprised that I had something to ask not only of my uncle but also of him.

He had set up a small room on the second floor of that house as his study. I had just left my uncle, and came up the stairs to find my father. When he saw me at the threshold of the office, he took his glasses off and looked up from the medical journal he was reading.

Did you have a good talk with your uncle? he said.

You could say that, I said.

I'm glad, my father said.

Does Amma know? I asked him. Did you believe that he would do something to your family?

She doesn't know, my father said. Why would I tell her? I was going to marry her anyway. Gambling on her meant gambling on him. I told you, you marry into a family—all of it. I didn't even know if he would tell you.

How long does he have? I asked.

A few months, my father said. You can hear whatever he has to say.

Don't you have anything to say? I asked him.

He closed the journal and looked up at me. Not really, he said. I married your mother, after all. I won, in a way.

How did you know that he wouldn't do anything? They can find people, I said. I've read about this. Even in North America, the Tigers find people and get them to donate money to the cause. I know that some people do it willingly, but I know that some of them are extorted. I know that they let him go in part because they think he'll raise support for the Tigers here. How did you know that it would be all right?

I had to think that it would be all right, he said. He smiled, which made him look a decade younger than he actually was. In the village where I grew up, he said, I had to fight for the things I wanted. I was the youngest and I had no father. I grew up cautiously, and when I met your mother, I did not want to be cautious anymore. America is not a cautious country. I felt safe enough to gamble, you see, and I had found something, someone, worth gambling on. I don't think I ever really thought he would do anything, even if he could. Can you imagine that? Really doing something? To someone from the place where you were born? Someone who loved your sister, and whom your sister loved? Considering my own family and my own history, I could not imagine that. In our way, my family did everything for Love. Maybe that was naive or foolish, but the places where we were born, your uncle and I—they are not so far apart, even if that is what he would have liked to believe, back when he thought I was not good enough for your mother. Even our philosophies are not so far apart—that the Tigers are right that a cruel government, a government that gets away with everything because it is a government, has wronged Tamils in Sri Lanka. I am a doctor, and I cannot agree with the Tigers' tactics, but at the end of the day, I am a Tamil. People attacked my friends, and the government let them. The government burned my library and attacked my village and took over my house, the house my father built for Love. I left my house and my family there, and the Sri Lankan Army moved in. So I can forgive your uncle, and maybe even understand him. The question is if you can.

I thought you didn't have anything to say, I said.

He was quiet for a moment, and then he reached up and turned off the lamp over his desk. He laughed.

Funny kid, he said, and that second word made him sound very American. You know better than that. All right: I thought I came to the West so that you would not have to know these things. So that you would not have to decide where you stand. But I think now that maybe that is impossible, because it's a war that belongs as much to you as to me. And you cannot decide where you stand unless you know all of it.

I WAS BORN LUCKY: I have a father. And so I am writing of Murali, not yet my father; Vani, not yet my mother; Janani, not yet a bride; and Kumaran, not yet gone. I do not know that my father, having fallen in Love, would see me married in the way that Janani has chosen. Nor do I know for certain what her father would say now, although there was a time when he stood against the changing of traditions. What made Kumaran someone who would set his weight against a moving world? What made my mother tell her family that they had to learn to love the man she loved? What made my father unafraid? My uncle's death is still fresh enough that we cannot look at Janani without thinking of him. Our fathers are nothing and everything alike. A long time ago, my father chose a path that led him out of Jaffna and to my mother. I cannot tell you whether Kumaran chose his way, but whether it was fated or willed, his path led to his absence from the temple of Janani's wedding—a certain space where a father should be.

I want to tell you why I am standing here beside a girl who is about to be Married, whose dead father tried to stop my parents from getting Married. I want to tell you why she is standing before a priest, and I am not. But don't think you can get the whole story. That's part of the charm. Voyage inside a family, and there will always be something unknown, a masked love or hatred, an unexplained death, the exact fragrance of the temple's air at the last wedding. That unknown could have been one person's beginning or another person's end. Marriage Without Consent, In-Love Marriage, is called something else, rendered into Propriety by sheer force of will. Don't think you can find out the truth about your family by coming in, exiting, and reentering through a back door of history, borrowing the record keeper's excuse for intruding with a pen. Even family members will not feel they owe you more than memory, which is convenient, and which has been made beautiful, often through falsehood. At the most, you can pull back the veil for a moment. But the imagination of a family can be as real as its history. Let me be clear: I am only one person. In mapping a family we draw blood from each other. I enter my family as I would a dream—with great caution and wonder.

There are those few who drop their guard, who let you enter. These are the people who have loved their lives enough to forget that you are there while they talk about what has happened to them. We are composed of those around us. Everyone's life is like a garden of relatives. *This is how I met the person I loved the most. This is how I loved the person I loved the most. This is how I lost the person I loved the most. This was my mother. This was my father.* They might as well be talking to themselves. They lose themselves in the pleasure of the sound of their own voices, the pictures of their own childhoods fresh again in their heads. They are there again, perfectly alone. A sublime solitude. I do not even have to say: *Forget I am listening. I am not even here. Tell me about my father, my mother, my uncle, my cousin.*

I meant to tell you about your mother, not about me, my uncle says, stopping in the midst of a story, so surprised at himself that he is out of breath.

But I find you just as interesting.

It's just one person's story. There are so many stories.

Translated, he is saying that his story does not matter. We both know this is a lie.

But: I can collect as many as I like, I say.

My uncle pauses. As long as you don't try to build any meaning or unity into it.

I'll try to stop myself.

He laughs. That would be a construction, he says. The reality is always more complex.

What he means is this: it would be false to say that there is a beginning to the story, or a middle, or an end. Those words have a tidiness that does not belong here. Our lives are not clean. They begin without fanfare and end without warning. This story does not have a defined shape or a pleasant arc. To record it differently would not be true.

[ondu]

MURALI

NOT YET MY FATHER

Let the physician inquire into the nature of the disease,
its cause and its method of cure, and treat it faithfully.

—TIRUKKURAL, *chapter 95, line 8*

MURALI: HE, TOO, GREW UP WITHOUT A FATHER.

He was only seven when Inspector Jegan died, and after that, almost in revenge—although upon whom he could not have told you—he remembered everything about his father. Everything. The lengths of their comparative shadows on their daily walks to and from the village school. How much money he had given to the temple. The imprints of his toes in his *ceruppu*, his slippers, in which Murali's own feet were far too small. His insistence on a mango after the evening meal. How his thick hair curled into an S at the nape of his neck when he needed a haircut.

Later, Murali took his father's name, Jegan, as his own, becoming J. Murali in a country that asked for two names. The inspector had once differentiated his father from the other Jegan, the Jegan who worked as a postmaster. Ariyalai was a big village, with two ends that were a few miles apart. In between, there were thousands of people—families in big houses, no one house too far from the others. They all knew the difference between Inspector Jegan and Postmaster Jegan, although perhaps none so well as Murali.

Inspector Jegan was a fearsome, smileless man, with hair that was already white when he died, although he had not reached fifty. He had heart trouble, like Murali, so when he walked down Kandy Road, which runs through Ariyalai and to Jaffna town, he walked steadily rather than quickly. Children not his own scattered out of his path. He was tall and thin, and in the Ariyalai sun his shadow was even taller. His children studied, and studied, and studied. He scolded other children he saw playing cricket, or loitering in the paths and nooks on the road—they should have been studying too. Although he scolded them, they snuck off to the movies, or to the *kadai* to buy a rupee's worth of sweets. His own children did not go to the movies. Their father thought the stories, imported from India, were too sexual—inappropriate for children. Every day, he walked a kilometer down the road to bring Murali home from the village primary school. He did not smile, never in photographs, or even at his youngest son, who watched for him through the window of the classroom with an anxious face. It was the steadiness of Jegan's expression that said what he meant. Murali was the eighth of eight children who loved their father not despite his famous strictness but because of it. Their father held an umbrella of care over them. He had built them a house with too-tall ceilings—a house that meant he expected them to grow. When Jegan died of a heart attack in his sleep, Murali dreamed of the monsoon blowing that house inside out.

IT DID RAIN ON THE DAY of Jegan's funeral, but gently—not hard enough to put out the fire of his body burning.

It was an enormous funeral, and everyone came, really everyone. Jegan's family was vast—Murali's father had had forty-six cousins alone. The cousins came, with their parents and their children. The aunts and the uncles came, including the ones who were not related, but whom Jegan's family had called aunts and uncles because they loved each other. All the government clerks who had worked for Jegan sat in a neat row in the back of the crowd, in front of a line of bicycles beyond the gates. And Tharshi, Murali's mother, surveyed this crowd of people. This was the first funeral at Chitupathi, a newly cleared field intended for Ariyalai's dead. Jegan had been given this honor because everyone had loved him.

His body was burned in the best spot, under a *maram*, a tree, which stood on the top of a slight hill. That morning, one of Jegan's brothers had come to the house and cut down an old tree there—a tree Jegan had nurtured for a long time with little success, a short one in its last years of green. Now his brother brought the wood, split it into long pieces, and laid it in a heap, so heat would gather at its center. The men of the family brought the body in a coffin and laid it on top of the wood, and Murali's oldest brother, Neelan, lit a torch. Then, looking away, he laid the fire to the wood. The body burned. The prayers had already been said.

Murali cried quietly, rubbing at his little face with his fists. They had not meant to let him come to the cremation grounds, but he had not had to insist on his right to be there because no one had remembered to argue with him. No one had told him what was happening, but he knew his father was dead. He was dressed in white mourning-clothes, like all of his brothers and sisters. He clutched some hibiscus flowers, the only brightness.

Flowers were not the custom, but he had snatched them off a bush his father had liked on his way to the field, and no one had stopped him. His thin back pressed up against his mother's knees, the misty dampness gathering in his hair, trickling down his face, onto his seven-year-old shoulders, through to his toes. The cold moved into him, although it was never really cold in Sri Lanka, even when it rained, even in Nuwara Eliya, even on the heights of the mountains.

Murali became still then, so still he almost forgot himself.

The next day, Murali's brother came to collect the ashes, which he took to the northernmost beach, in Point Pedro, where Jegan drifted into the ocean, and away.

ARIYALAI STOPPED BURNING its dead at Chitupathi many decades later, when the field became too mine-laden, a result of the war between the Tamil militants and the Sri Lankan Army. Later still, the replacement site, Chemmani, became the site of a massacre of Tamil civilians, and Ariyalai returned to a demined Chitupathi. Murali heard this from around the world and remembered standing in that field, remembered himself in medical school, and understood, finally, how much dignity a cadaver might have in its very intactness.

Even now, he still has the *malaranjali*, the memorial book from his father's funeral. It crossed the ocean with him, tucked in an inside pocket of his suitcase. Like all memorial books, it contains the lineage of the deceased. Murali holds on to it, remembering its making. The writer, a neighboring scholar, had wanted to include Jegan's father's name. But in that whole vast family, no one had known the name of the long-dead, unmet grandfather. They asked the uncles, the aunts, the brothers, the sisters—but no one knew, and it was not a question Tharshi had ever thought to ask. Not something wives asked in a place where there are no real last names. Names were not passed down from father to son, as they are in America. And so Tharshi—Jegan's own wife—did not know.

It had taken a long time before anyone thought to ask Murali. After all, he was only seven years old. He had loved his father; he had stood very still, so still he had forgotten himself, and others had forgotten him also. He had been the only one with the answer. Jegan was his father; Jegan's father was Kathiravelu. Murali knew because he had spent so much time with his father on those walks to and from school. He knew, because as small boys do, he had asked his father questions that neither of them considered very important, just for the sake of hearing his father talk. It was only later, you see, that the question was important.

Became important. He was just Murali, once. A young boy who, after his father's death, tried to stop himself from being young. Now he and his brothers have added their father to their names. All of them Jegan.

At home in Sri Lanka, my father says, we do things differently. We do not bear our ancestors all our lives. They are only written down when we die.

Murali: the reed-thin, dark boy stood alone in a field where ashes had lain and bombs would fall. And so he grew up unafraid of either.

MURALI: HE WAS THE YOUNGEST, and he had no father. But he had a mother. What a mother! Even the priests at the local Ganesha temple called her "one of the best women." They did not say "kindest," or "most beautiful." Best, they said: best. They anointed her forever with that word because of how deeply they meant it. By the time her husband died, her youth was long past, if measured in children, but not so distant if measured in years. Once she had been a *pala-pundithai*—a novice pundit. But then his father, Jègan, who was from the opposite side of the village, saw her recite at a school competition.

Jegan, not yet my grandfather, came to one of the school functions, which were popular in the town, even with those who did not have young children. Ariyalai took a collective pride in their accomplished students. On that occasion, Tharshi made them feel this especially. Everyone in the audience thought she resembled them. And she did resemble all of them, because she knew the village and loved it and brought it with her wherever she went. She carried herself well, unlike some of the other girls, who walked with their shoulders pulled forward to hide new breasts. No one had yet convinced her to be ashamed, and this quality called out to Jegan. He saw how tall she was and how she threw her head back. He saw the long, long line of her throat and her black braid. He had not seen her in a long time, or perhaps it was just that he had not recognized her as the woman to whom he would belong.

But there was something in between, something that Tharshi felt and never said to Jegan: she should not have been the one standing on that stage. He had seen a face he could love, but that face belonged to two women.

EVERYONE IN ARIYALAI WALKED in pairs, except for Tharshi. No one felt too sorry for her, although her husband had died and left her with eight children. She had already been loved. Although this is a story my father now knows, he has chosen not to believe in the patterns of fate, as his mother did. But Tharshi had a twin, a sister, and when she stood on the stage at the ladies' college in Jaffna to give her recitation, she was standing in a place she did not consider her own.

At this annual recital, the young women of the college sang and declaimed passages from various scholarly and holy texts. The students competed for a prize of some money, which was to be used for books. The twins, Thevayani and Tharshi, were twelve that year. They both looked older. They were ravishingly nearly identical, both of them with strong-boned oval faces, long braids, almond-shaped, tilted eyes, high brows, and stubborn mouths. Thevayani, called Kunju, was the elder by four minutes only, and a little bit taller, but the only person who could unfailingly tell them apart was their father, the widower Ragavan. Of the two of them, Kunju was the smarter, and Tharshi the quieter. Each one walked with the confident grace Ragavan remembered in their dead mother. Both of them wanted to be *pala-pundithai;* they loved to read and wanted to enter that year's competition: Kunju, as one of the school's top students, thought she might win it. Their father told them that he thought only one of them should participate in the contest; he did not like the idea of sisters competing against each other. They both looked at him hopefully. Who would he choose? He paused and sighed. Preventing them from competing meant that he had to favor one of them.

He hesitated and looked at them, these two lovely daughters of his. Both of them so much like him. He told them that he thought it should be Kunju, because she had a real chance of winning. They needed the money.

THARSHI DID NOT HOLD A GRUDGE—not one to which she or anyone else would admit. She listened to her sister practice until the recitation was perfect. One day, one week before the competition, the two of them decided to do a rehearsal in full dress. Tharshi lent her sister her own diamond jewelry: earrings, a necklace, and a *mūkkutti*, a stud for her nose. She had woven a garland with hibiscus from the garden, and she plaited it into Kunju's long rope of hair. Their father had given Kunju one of their mother's saris to wear. It was her first real sari—an honor for someone her age, who usually wore only the school uniform, a plain dress, or a half-sari. Now, Tharshi ironed her mother's silk for her sister to wear. Kunju wound the bolt of cloth around herself. She did not have a practiced hand, or a mother, so she remade the pleats again and again until the folds lay crisp and perfect, flat against her waist. She slid the heavy gold bangles onto her wrist, twisted the *mūkkutti* where it shone, a bright diamond star flaring in her strong-boned nose. Tharshi patted a stray curl into place and pulled at the sari until it hung just right on her sister's taller, more elegant frame.

Because the recitation in question was a holy passage, they walked to the local temple to practice. From the veranda of their house, their father watched them walking, hand in hand. He had to remind himself that they were only twelve. Ravishingly nearly identical, and not.

GANESHA, THE GOD OF scholars and luck, looked down on Kunju, blessing her studies, and she spoke well. From the corners of the temple, the priests, attending to their tasks of washing and dressing the gods, listened to her and blessed her also. Kunju was dazzling, of course, and watching her Tharshi was sure she would steal the show, win the prize, all of that. How could she not? What kind of story would this be? Tharshi's diamonds glimmered on Kunju as she gestured grandly. Her voice was clear and sweet. She would not need anything to make it clearer. In her mind, Tharshi saw it unfold: the women in the first row sobbing into their handkerchiefs, and the men coughing to hide how much she moved them. Afterward, the judges would nod sagely among themselves, trading cigarettes and muttering to one another that Ragavan *machan*'s little girl was really something.

NOT EVERYTHING GOES ACCORDING to plan. Certainly not Marriage. That night when Tharshi and Kunju came home, flushed with the anticipation of Kunju's success, they took the lamp inside the hall to say their prayers. As Kunju set the oil lamp down on the mat on the floor in front of the household shrine, the edge of her mother's sari caught in the flame. It ran up the silk like a long-legged and hungry spider, licked at her long braid, edged toward her face and wide dark eyes. It wound around her waist like a caressing hand and lit her body up her slender throat to her face.

Later, in her memory, Tharshi always saw the fire in slow motion, moving at a speed at which she could have stopped it. But what really happened was that Tharshi saw her mirror image burning in front of her, consumed by light, like a small sun. The sound of the scream was a nightmare distortion, the voice in which Kunju had spoken so clearly earlier that evening twisted into a different, horrible shape. Tharshi too screamed and screamed, hearing rather than feeling the sound of her own footsteps as she ran to the well and called for her father.

IT TOOK A LONG TIME before Kunju healed. She never really did. Such severe burns usually leave scars. Kunju, who had been prized for her beauty, was badly disfigured. And, of course, the twins were never again identical. Her color had changed, the shape of her full-lipped mouth altered. It was almost unbearable to look at them standing next to each other. The fire had burned Kunju's right arm so that it was nearly purple, almost bone. The flames had touched her face, twisting her left cheek and changing the outline of one eye. Ragavan looked at his older daughter, his most-loved-by-four-minutes daughter, and wept. What would happen to her? The only part of her face that still moved were those dark eyes. He could not bear to look into them. Kunju would need special attention for the rest of her life. Her face a burden to the men who might have married her.

It should have been Kunju on that stage. *Dearest. Darling. Beloved.* That was what her name meant. The truth was that he loved her more. Tharshi and Kunju were identical twins. They were the same. But Not. We lie both to and because of the people we love the most.

AND IT HAPPENED AS Tharshi had seen it would: her voice was clear and sweet, ringing to the corners of the big hall without anything to make it louder. The women in the first row sobbed into their handkerchiefs, and the men coughed to hide how much she moved them. She became Kunju, spoke like Kunju, threw her head back like Kunju. And afterward, the judges nodded sagely among themselves, trading cigarettes and muttering to one another that Ragavan *machan*'s little girl was really something. Others in the audience were impressed too. One in particular. Jegan had attended the concert on impulse, but now, he thought, his eyes riveted to Tharshi's sharply cut face, he was very glad he had chosen this.

Jegan wrote his life like a novel. Or perhaps, because the novel is not originally a Tamil form, an epic poem. He fell in love not with the girl on the stage, but with who he saw her becoming, how her voice promised that she would grow into a certain kind of woman. Just as years later, Murali saw Vani's future in the structure of her face, falling in love with her and her next self. Tharshi was only twelve. But if Jegan closed his eyes, he could see her life unfolding next to his. He loved the independence of her carriage. She would never need him, and he did not want her to need him.

INSTEAD OF SENDING HIS own family, as was the custom, Jegan went to see her father himself the next day. The difference between the two men was striking: Jegan, with his wide-set eyes and light brown skin, was dressed nicely. A government man. Ragavan was a farmer. Jegan looked about the house with curiosity and Ragavan held his breath.

When Jegan explained to him why he had come, Ragavan began to nod slowly. He could not say yes all at once, of course, but what Jegan was asking could eventually come to pass. It was almost too good to be true, that this man wanted to marry Tharshi and thought her so beautiful. But Ragavan could not help but remember that Kunju slept alone in a back room, her face burned too dry for tears. Looking at Jegan, Ragavan saw fortune and tasted ashes.

THARSHI BOWED HER BLACK head to her father's decree that she would marry Jegan. Kunju smiled with the half of her face that still could. She had heard the conversation between her father and Jegan. He would pay for the rest of Tharshi's education, and she would become the wife of a government man. All of these things would become her sister's: the prize, the education, the husband, and the distant promise of a prominent house in their village.

After the first week, Kunju began to refuse to let Tharshi, who had nursed her, rub her scars with oil. Tharshi began to sleep in another room, abandoning the one they had shared. Alone in a dark room, Kunju applied the oil herself, unscrewing the cap of the bottle with tiny, measured twists. And every day she moved another inch. One day she lifted her arms up and lowered them. Another day she reached for the curtain to let in some light. After a while, she rehearsed walking. Slowly she resumed her household duties, each of which took her twice as long with her new stiffness. Tharshi watched her and said nothing, and Kunju burned inside with something she did not want to name. Although everyone knew what had happened, and some of their relatives had even tried to visit her, she had refused them, and so no one had seen her.

And then finally, because she knew she had to do it, and because Ragavan made her, she left the house to walk through the village.

HER FATHER ASKED HER to do an errand in the village for him one day, and at first she just stared blankly at his request. His mouth crumpled and he called for Tharshi. Kunju reached out her burned hand and touched his arm to stop him. He flinched. She saw him flinch, and it hurt her. She put her hurt away and pretended that she had not seen him recoil.

I'll go, she said.

Earlier she had asked her father to remove her small mirror from her room. Now she went into her sister's room—Tharshi was not at home—and looked at her reflection in the glass. If she was to go out she could not hide her face, and she would not try to do so. She pinned her hair back. Her damaged face was unmasked, revealed. Her ears were marked with ragged holes in the places where Tharshi's diamonds earrings had been cut out. Her skin was like the color of coal after it has been burned. She went out and down into the village.

As she walked through the main road she could almost hear those around her stopping and their heads turning. Because the change was so startling, her face drew people even more now than it had when she was beautiful. It had lost the ability to admit color or shame and so the people who stared at her did not know what she was feeling. Her mouth did not move. Her eyebrow was frozen in a scarred arch that could have been angry or questioning. She felt as though she were still on fire, but that now it was the eyes of the people around her that burned. They were coldly curious and warmly pitying. They were eyes she had known all her life and they did not recognize her.

When she came back with what her father had asked her to bring, he was waiting for her in the doorway. She looked up at him and their eyes met. He reached out and touched her face for the first time since it had changed. Her cheek was rough now. She had forgotten what it felt like to be touched. She knew that when she crossed the threshold, it would be for the last time. She could not bear to leave again. She could not bear that people had seen her like this. Her face was irrevocably undone. She was irrevocably alone.

Kunju made her grief something unseen. Every day she lived with it, breathed it, and tasted its sour bouquet. Every day she loved her sister. Every day she hated her sister. And three years later, Ragavan took Tharshi to marry Jegan, and Kunju was alone in the house where they had grown up together. Twins.

JEGAN AND THARSHI WERE almost a generation apart. They did not care. Simply and easily, Tharshi loved Jegan, and he loved her. This is the way Arranged Marriages should work. She never told him who was meant to be standing on the stage that night, but he had heard her sister's story all around the village. Was she the twin fate had meant for him? Who was to say? She was the wrong twin, but the right wife. It could not be undone, because it was something no one had done. When Jegan died, Tharshi stood at his memorial at the tree on the top of the hill and threw her head back, once more unconsciously imitating the sister whose beauty and voice might have caught his unknowing Heart long ago, had things been different. By the time he died, Tharshi's braid had turned snow-white, even though her face was still a schoolgirl's, unlined and fresh. Her life had taken an unpredictable turn when he entered it; her Heart had bent unexpectedly to receive him. As he had foreseen, he married a girl, and she became a woman who did not need him. She would go on to raise his children without him. But she loved him. Two people she loved consumed by fire.

THARSHI: ALTHOUGH SHE DID not say this to her children, they saw that she felt that their father's death was part of the order of things. She shared their sorrow, but not their anger. It was only later that Murali understood that she thought Jegan's early death was payment for her marrying him. A debt owed and settled. Ariyalai was a town full of fathers who took special pride in their sons. And now her fatherless son Murali tried to become a doctor. Not the kind of doctor who brought prayers and herbs—the kind who thought precisely, the kind who measured and watched and trusted nothing he did not see. Even then, Murali did not believe in fate or *ayurvedam.* He wanted something of which he was sure: science.

He dreamed of cardiology. He was thinking of the cautious little boy he had been. He was thinking of his father dying in the night, and his mother waking up as though she had expected it. He was thinking of his family and their collection of Hearts. But he was told that this was not a fruitful profession. Live in a grittier reality than that of hearts, of blood, they said. At first he did not want to, but then he thought: oncology.

In choosing this science, he realized only later, he chose not only one fork of a clinical path, but a permanent fealty to the landscape of his childhood. A place where anything could fail, and where any illness illuminated a failure to foresee. This was not only about blood; it was about an entire body's capacity for betrayal. It was not only about a valve or an artery granting or denying admittance. This was about survival, an assemblage of parts. It required planning. A cancer, like a cloud, could fade gradually into the distance—or blossom, its subtlest increase untracked by the careless eye. The faintest breeze could move it a millimeter to be paid for years later. To the oncologist, everything was a potential minefield to be analyzed and dissected, the body merely another bomb anticipating explosion. He learned to approach the body in the same manner he would a bomb, knowing that the error was always tangible. He had learned to love the acquisition of knowledge, how one could assemble the skeleton of disease from the bones of symptoms. A body could fluctuate and even crumble with temper and stress, but its failure in the end was more often pure and intricate mechanics. Controllable. Fixable. This, then, he would learn to manipulate, as he had never been able to manipulate his own body. Oncology, requiring a total mastery, ending in the throb and thrum of a heartbeat he could steady.

Murali chose this as his profession, but entering medical school in Sri Lanka was not easy. There were only two hundred and fifty students admitted every year, and one hundred times that number took the entrance exams. He was a member of Sri Lanka's ethnic Tamil minority, and this meant that to enter he had to score even higher. There were quotas. Like everyone else, he failed the first time and was neither greatly surprised nor disappointed. He took the test again the next year and passed.

The university he chose was far away from Ariyalai, at Peradeniya, near Kandy, in the high, cool mountains. He took the train there, alone, a slim brown boy with a slim brown suitcase that was enough to hold all the clothes he owned. He walked from the station to the campus, alone, and the day was so bright that he squinted. He registered and took the slim brown suitcase to the room they had assigned him. It was a tiny space, and he did not bother to unpack, seeing how, later, he would slam his hips, his back, his elbows into plaster walls so narrow.

He went downstairs, still alone, because the other students had not yet arrived. He had been one of the first; he liked to be early, to see the lay of the land before entering it. The main hall looked bare and hot, and big with emptiness. He held his breath almost automatically, suddenly unsure of himself here. He was only eighteen years old. But if he closed his eyes and listened, he could hear his Heart murmuring, and the memory of his Heart murmuring.

THEY MADE THE FIRST fortnight of medical school hell. Later he would understand why, remembering his revulsion at the sight of the first cadaver. If he was distracted with other things, the rituals of initiations and the macabre humor of young men, he could not think too deeply about his interaction with the ex-person before him. And you had to think of him or her as an ex-person to learn the tender caress of the scalpel, to see how a knife could navigate a spine, lift away skin, reveal muscle and tendon. All bodies are alike in certain facets of their geometry, and for a doctor to understand that, the body had to be everyone and no one. *A person (formerly)* was how Murali thought of it, the descriptive always added like that: an afterthought bracketed by parentheses. He had carried his own dead father with him for many years in his Heart, and this burden was not easily put aside. He found in dissection and study a strange intimacy with these dead, who were not his dead, but the dead of someone else. Many of the other students had never seen a dead body before and stood before their assignments agape and fascinated. Some of them were ill. He heard the sounds of them vomiting in the hall as though from a great distance. He had seen his own father's peaceful face when he was quite young, and he thought about that as he stood over his first body, his face impassive. This was the first test: look at the body and make it no one. A person. (Formerly.)

He had been assigned what they called a body partner, another boy from Jaffna named Murugan who was his friend and colleague by virtue of having been next to him in the alphabetical class lists for years. Neither one of them became ill during this first procedure, and neither one of them spoke. There was no formal or verbal guidance for the first hours. You were alone with the body; you became acquainted. It was during these three hours, before the instructors arrived, that he learned to love the body. He had always seen it as flawed, perhaps because the first body he had met was his own. Those innumerable possibilities for disaster. A thousand parts, none of which were infallible. But over the course of those three hours in the silent hall, he saw for the first time how perfectly everything could work. The synchrony of limb and ligament, the elegance of a joint. A hand he could shake, that would not shake back. *How are you, sir,* he thought politely. *(Formerly Sir.)* How nice to meet the body! These fingers had been broken once. He touched them with his own gloved fingers, matching them up and seeing that the hands were very large, larger than his own. *Perhaps they were broken when you were young?* he thought. *You have a scar on your neck—did you cut yourself while shaving, or perhaps during a fight? I see that you were going bald, that you had diabetes and smoked, that you favored your right leg, that you were married, that someone loved you.* The ring was still on the cadaver's dead finger. Murali thought all of this quite calmly, smelling vaguely the scent of eau de cologne behind him; they were using it to revive a student who had fainted. Murali himself had long ago given up the practice of fainting, despite his illness: it was a matter of principle.

In this country, at this time, the practice of initiations was not called hazing, but "ragging." It was a more civilized word, perhaps. Murali watched and participated in what was happening because he had no choice, but also because in spite of himself he was mesmerized. He began to think that he could imagine what addiction would be like: like ragging, or watching someone being ragged. It required the kind of force he had never had or wanted in himself. But these people were not cruel. He knew that he too would do whatever the senior medical students told him to do, and that it would not be difficult. Later, as a father, as my father, he might worry about hazing. But for now, there was only the cold face below him.

Murali, one senior said to him, and he looked up through a formaldehyde haze, his gloves dripping saline.

Yes, sir, he responded promptly and politely, anticipation like sugarcane sweet in his mouth.

Go over there to the girl at cadaver number seven, and propose to her.

Murali put his scalpel down. The girl at number seven looked at him, a brittle bone cracking as she moved the arm of her cadaver, folding its hands neatly on its breast. All right, he told himself, all right. He was sure they had warned her in advance. Murugan looked at him expectantly. The long hall, which had been buzzing with students, paused to watch the spectacle. The girl kept picking up her scalpel and putting it down again, making a tracery of cuts up the shoulder of her cadaver, nervous at being the center of attention. He knew her slightly, and his eyes apologized before he even spoke. Then he grinned cheerfully.

How are you? he asked her.

Fine, fine, she said, still embarrassed. She fingered an earring.

You look very beautiful in your lab coat, he offered.

She giggled, surprised in spite of herself.

Will you marry me? He made sure to say it loud enough for everyone to hear.

She giggled again and paused before delivering her answer: Yes.

AFTER MEDICAL SCHOOL HE never saw her again, although he always thought of her affectionately as his Practice Proposal. Nothing was ever so easy again as those first three naked hours. The same people who had failed their entrance exams on the first try were all too likely to fail their final exams and have to spend an extra six months in school before they could try again. Murali was determined not to be one of these. He thought he understood this, finally, the body and its machinations. But he wanted to be sure. In the weeks before the test, he cloistered himself in the library, his dark head bent over his books. His was only one dark head in a row of many dark heads.

The written exams were not the hardest part of the test, and everyone knew this. The real complication was the clinical test, in which the student was presented with three patients. He would be allowed to spend three quarters of an hour with each of them, and then another quarter of an hour making a presentation on diagnosis and suggested course of treatment. You had to be very careful to divide the first part of the hour to allow for both a case history and an examination: the body in the patient's words and then in your own. It sounded simple enough when the structure of the test was explained, but Murali knew this was only a deception. They went out of their way to find people with obscure diseases. This was not difficult for them; they spent their days teaching and their nights on charity work in the surrounding villages. When the time for the tests came, the instructors went to the village markets, the rice fields, the small offices, and retrieved their own strangest patients. These people had bodies that were constantly failing in innovative and mysterious ways. Not all of them spoke English; they were mostly Sinhalese, and although you were permitted a translator, there was no extra time allotted for such an extravagance. Murali vowed not to need one.

His first patient was a girl who was extremely beautiful, and unmistakably barren. This was easy enough to diagnose, and he was relieved not to face the burden of disclosure; he saw soon enough that she already knew. He moved on to the next patient, a man whose kidneys were dysfunctional, and in this case too, he finished in advance and saw his instructors smiling with approval. He heaved a dry breath as they took him to the third patient; he knew that tradition required that the third patient be the most difficult, and this was the last fence he had to leap to pass. The patient was a boy, not much younger than himself, but clearly much poorer. He hoisted himself onto the examining table, and Murali saw that even this small effort, lifting himself with his hands, tired him immeasurably. Murali recognized something in this fatigue, if only vaguely. The boy's small, unbendable frame was so tired and yet held so straight.

What is the matter? he asked. He gestured for the boy to lie down and listened as he probed with gentle fingers. The boy described an inability to breathe, and Murali's brain said *asthma?* No, that would have been too easy. People still sometimes contracted tuberculosis. The boy's breath hitched and jumped, and Murali pressed against his ribs. There, the boy said, and Murali uneasily decided he had cracked ribs and perhaps a punctured lung. He felt a rumble begin in his belly; he had been unable to eat this morning because of nervousness, and now the feeling, which had been only hunger before, expanded so that it seemed to hold all of him inside a bubble of uncertainty. He recognized something about this boy, and he could not put words to it. He did not like to see this: unnamable flaws, untraceable tracks. Bodies did not work like that; the failing was not just in the patient, but in the doctor. He ought to be able to see what it was. Errors of the body were tangible.

When he told his instructors his final diagnosis, they looked at him, brows cocked. Is that your final decision, Mr. Murali?

they asked. You have a quarter of an hour left to examine the patient.

But Murali knew that he would see nothing else; this patient's body had betrayed no more. Although something more might be there, a quarter of an hour would not be enough to find it. His hands had become sweaty and slipped as he replaced his stethoscope around his neck. He nodded slowly at them to indicate that he was finished, and his stomach lurched when he saw pair after pair of disappointed eyes.

We'll see you next term, Mr. Murali, said the head instructor.

What was it? Murali asked. What did I miss?

You were correct about the ribs and the punctured lung, but you missed a second, underlying diagnosis.

A door that had been locked in Murali's brain began to creak slowly open. He thought that he could see a bit of light around the corner.

You listened to his heartbeat, Murali, the older doctor said. I'm not sure why you didn't hear the murmur.

WHEN HE TOOK THE TEST again six months later, he passed the clinical portion with such high marks that a new examiner wanted to give him honors. But this wasn't allowed if you had already failed once before. It did not matter; the time had passed for him to care about this. He was preparing to leave the country, and the classmates and teachers he had learned to love.

In emigrating he would leave behind such things and people, the kind of friendly no-longer-strangers whose faces were like his own, whose gentle humor was really humour in the British and Sri Lankan way. Later he would miss this, the rich languid roundness of that British *U*, the caressed belly of a word on a British tongue. He had gone to school in English, but as a young man, he still thought in Tamil. Later, when he was older, he would find that the language of his dreams had changed. He dreamed in English, but not the American English of his daughter. He dreamed of that gentle wit, those British tongues, and the cold face of the cadaver below him. That perfect body.

It was language that did him in, language that in the end sent him on his way. He was required to take yet another test to be placed in a government hospital. It was a proficiency test in Sinhalese, which was the official language of the island and had been since 1956. The Tamil Language Act of 1958 had long been forgotten, and this was the reality. Only a few years later, Tamils would have to score higher on the test than their Sinhalese counterparts in order to continue their studies. He loved to speak his own language, but he spoke Sinhalese well and he was not worried about what the government required. But when he reported to the local test office and opened the booklet he felt blank and sick. The minutes on the clock ticked away, and he thought it was like the beating of his Heart, and he was sure that in the quiet room with all the medical students sweating, everyone could hear his brain racing at a liquid speed in Tamil. He had known Sinhalese his whole life, but now he lowered a pail into the well of his mind and found not a word. At the end of the exam he rose steadily and handed his clean paper to the examiner.

At the gate of the office, Murugan joined him and they walked up the road together, stopping at the public well. When they were younger they had walked this road barefoot. Now they were grown men, wearing covered loafers and long trousers. Their feet kicked up dust that made Murali cough. Murugan handed Murali the dipper of water. Murali gulped the water down, tipping the rest of it onto his head so that his hair was plastered to his brow. Murugan was watching him.

What did you think of the test?

I passed it, Murali said.

But it was hard, wasn't it, Murugan said, without a question mark. He was chewing betel leaf and he spit in the dirt next to Murali's foot.

I won't take another test in Sinhalese, Murali said and shrugged, suddenly angry.

What do you mean? Murugan stared.

I'm leaving this country, Murali said, surprised.

He was going. He was going. When he told his mother, she cried. She had never found him so immovable. She could not have known—as he did not either—that he was practicing immovability for a moment when he would really need it. He was making himself into a man who would Love my mother before Marrying her.

[rendu]

DEATH CREEPING TOWARD US

On her bright brow alone is destroyed even that power of mine that used to terrify the most fearless foes in the battlefield.

—TIRUKKURAL, *chapter 109, line 8*

SUTHAN: DECADES LATER, ANOTHER MAN, DECIDING TO MARRY another woman. Who knew if or when he would Love her? That was not what this was about. I saw him first about a week after my uncle's arrival, when he came with his father to the small house in Scarborough, Toronto.

We had been told that he was a few years older than I. He looked younger, perhaps because of the leanness of his silhouette. In the fashion of young men, he had grown a small patch of hair under his lower lip. His ears stuck out from the sides of his head slightly, emphasized by a close-cropped and uneven haircut, but even this could not disguise his essential handsomeness. He had a small mouth, from which a deep voice would eventually emerge. He came to the door and loomed behind his father, who had come to visit my father and my uncle. He kept his hands folded behind his back, not in his pockets, and standing in the doorway, I thought him very formal and quiet for someone our age, someone who had already secured a position of sorts in our family.

He resembled his father, although perhaps it only seemed so because his mother was not there. She had passed away some fifteen years ago, I knew. After I opened the door, his father leaned into the open air and studied me intently, and I realized that he thought that I was his future daughter-in-law.

Hello, uncle, I said in English.

Ah, then you are not Janani, he said. But he was still studying me. He smiled suddenly, and I remembered what my father had told me about this man. My uncle had still not said much about him, but my father, as always, told me the truth: exactly what he thought was true, no more and no less.

That man, Vijendran, he is a powerful man here in Toronto, my father said. Some of my relatives who live here in Toronto know this man, and they say that he has spent many years getting support for the Tigers here. This is not a hard thing to do, because most of the Tamils here came here after you were born. Canada offered them refuge after 1983. They have been angry for a long time because of what happened in the month when you were born. We mark that as our darkest hour. And is it so easy to blame those people, when they lost so much? Their homes? Their property? Their loved ones?

I had been born in 1983, in July, when thousands of Tamils were killed while their government did nothing, and I knew that I came from a generation of people who marked those dates as their blackest hour, even though some of us had not even been born yet. I knew that the son of Vijendran, this boy, Suthan, was one of those who held on to that date and all it meant; I knew that soon, Janani would come downstairs, wearing one of my mother's saris, to meet him, and that they would agree on many things, and that one of them would be the Tigers.

Come in, I said to Vijendran and Suthan, and they untied their shoes and left them at the door, as was the custom of Tamils even in the West.

I called for my mother, and she came out into the hall to meet them. My father followed behind her. They each shook hands with Vijendran, and then his son. Luck for a new Marriage in a new place.

TEA: THIS IS A CIVILIZING THING. In any country, in any time, tea brings order and calm to a place of chaos. And not every place of chaos looks like one. Two families in a too-clean parlor room in Toronto can be chaos.

And it was, I realized. The men—my father and Vijendran and Suthan—sat around a polished wooden table, and I went to the kitchen to help my mother to get the trays and cups. Sri Lankan women are always trying and failing to bring order to a world of men. My mother had taken out her Indian serving set: a small silver bowl of cashews; another of deep-fried noodles, spicy nuts, and lentils; a third of crispy *vadai*, the savory snack my father especially liked and that my mother had refused to prepare for him, because it was so unhealthy. But my mother had been expecting them, and they were important people, the kind for whom one prepared special things. In the kitchen, I watched my mother, the set of her shoulders, and her lips, which tightened at the corners. She did not like this man, Vijendran, and she did not like his son. It had taken me a long time to see behind the curtain of her politeness, and to see what she really thought about people. I had had to travel to another country to see what made her uncomfortable, to see what made her afraid.

She handed me the tray of food.

Ask them how they take their tea, she said to me, and leaned down to get the kettle from the cupboard.

I took the food back out into the living room, where I offered it to each man—first Vijendran, then his son, then my father—before setting it down on the table.

Where is your niece? Vijendran asked my father.

Go and call her, my father said to me.

But I did not have to. She came downstairs, wearing one of my mother's saris that was just right for the occasion: lavender, with subtle embroidery. She looked very tall, even without any shoes on, and even fairer than she had looked in the afternoon light at the airport, on that first day. I looked at Vijendran, who was smiling approvingly; I looked at his son, who looked stern and yet happy, without smiling. They both stood up, and I thought: that is what men of a certain era do in the presence of a lady. What time are we in? I wondered. When are we?

Janani looked down and smiled.

This is my niece, my father said.

I did not want to be a part of this, but I could not help but compare myself to her: darker, shorter, bigger. Less lovely. Less Sri Lankan, less proper. Less modest. I wore pants; I had cut my hair short at the beginning of the summer, and it had not yet grown out. Janani, I thought, looked like my mother. I was suddenly sure of it: that Janani, with all her knowledge of what violence could do or be, looked more like my peaceful, lovely mother than I ever had.

[mundu]

VANI

NOT YET MY MOTHER

What is not conferred by fate cannot be preserved,
although it be guarded with most painful care;
and that which fate has made his cannot be lost,
although one should undertake to throw it away.

—TIRUKKURAL, *chapter 38, line 6*

VANI: SHE STEPPED ONTO THE ESCALATOR VERY CAREFULLY because she had never seen one before. She counted under her breath, *one, two, three, four, one, two, three, four,* and placed her right foot and then her left, onto the moving shelf. She said to herself, I will go back. I will go back. She meant it. She had no intention of staying. This was Vani, not yet my mother, but stepping onto an airport escalator that would take her there.

Like Murali, she speaks excellent English, which is part of what brought her here. She went to a school where she was taught everything that way, in English. She learned what she was taught and learned it well. But she could not forget that each of her bones had emerged from a Tamil womb. Into a place and family that was Tamil.

It was a country that still remembered the British, who left the year she was born, which was the same year India gained independence. But even now, she still thinks in Tamil. She is exceedingly practical, and also very beautiful. In her world, beauty is a convenient and unimportant side note: Beautiful, but So What? She was not always beautiful—Vani, not yet my mother. Once she was just a little girl in Urelu, another village of Jaffna. Today it is not far from Ariyalai, but then it was far enough that she and Murali never crossed paths. In Urelu, she was not known for athleticism, as her older sister was. She was not known for temper or politics, as Kumaran was. She was not yet known for beauty—after all, she was not yet Beautiful-So-What.

She was the youngest of the children, of which there were three. My aunt Kalyani was born first; second, my uncle Kumaran, the precious boy; and lastly, my mother, Vani. She was good; that was what she was. She was clean and methodical and she never wasted a moment. She is still like this: single-minded. Her name means "wish" or "desire," which is entirely appropriate. My mother was not born lucky. Luck is something that happens to you. Nothing merely *happens* to my mother. This connotes a kind of passivity that is foreign to her; she does not understand or yield to it. She has created the situation around her through the strength of her will.

Although I know that she intended to return, I can only guess at why she left Sri Lanka to come to America; unlike the departure of my father, hers has remained an untold story. My mother is not a teller of stories. I realize this about my mother now, her natural reticence, which is not reticence exactly, but rather an almost completely unself-conscious manner of being, a lack of ego that is total in this facet. It does not occur to her to talk about herself. There is simply no reason to do so, and my mother does not often do things without a reason. Her entire family is like this.

Tell me about what my mother was like, I say to a relative on my mother's side of the family.

You don't need to know that, she says in return.

I know this: when she left Sri Lanka, a busful of relatives came to the station to say good-bye to her. When she left, she was in her mid-twenties, not yet beautiful but beginning to be so, not yet my mother, but closer to being so. She was learning a kind of independence she had never imagined, and it was also a kind of independence that she did not want: freedom from her family, which was the thing she loved the most, and which was what she later became known for, at least to me, her daughter. Her love for her family and the life they had led. She was going away, to another country, because she had managed to get a visa, and she knew that this was no longer a good place to be, although it had been a good place to her all her life. She was going, she told herself and her relatives, only for two years. But perhaps somewhere deep down she knew she would never come back.

She had chosen to become a teacher because she liked to

teach children, and she loved children themselves, their striving toward character. But this was no longer a good place to teach, or (she thought but did not say) to have children. The teachers at her convent school had gotten her an assignment to teach in New York City. A busful of her relatives came to the airport to see her off. She kissed them good-bye and wished they could come with her. She did not consciously desire disconnection. There was a particular sacredness about everything she had been able to do here. This was something she saw only as she left. The only moment in which you understand an entire perspective is as you look over your shoulder to say good-bye, and this was true for my mother also. The sacred quality of this place was not a holiness she ascribed to herself but rather to everything around her, all the people who had been kind to her, the nuns who had taught her from her time in the convent school as a small girl to her training as a teacher, her family that had sheltered and loved her because she was the youngest, and not because she was especially known for anything but just being Vani, which was enough for them.

She saw now, for the first time, that it might not be enough for anyone else. She was leaving a very religious family, a family that was very tight-knit and traditional. It was and is a family that honors ceremony and resists separation. If this family saw the earth open up in its midst, my mother and her siblings would deny it and then fight to fill the chasm. This is both admirable and self-destructive. My mother is someone who could see a fire in front of her and say it was not there. My mother is someone who, by the force of her will, could put a fire out.

MY MOTHER'S FAMILY IDENTIFIES itself first by honor, although they do not call it that. They do not call it anything, but it is the unnamed honor of a murdered man. I did not know he had been murdered because when they spoke of him they used his name to wrap around the entire family: you are a Vairavan, they would say, and I did not know that they meant him, because when I was born he had been dead for a long time. He had surpassed the boundaries of his life to take over all of theirs. They had named their essential bond after him. He was my mother's grandfather, her mother's father. She was six years old when he died. It was 1954. It was their introduction to violence.

He was sixty-three when he was killed. He had been such a good man that even years later, they spoke about him always as though he were still alive. They never spoke about his unusual passing. Why would they? It did not matter—the mere *how* of his death. Its story had no reason. Who cared for the how? They cared far more about the kind of man he had been. Later, I was told that he was killed because he was so good. I think this is something that his children chose to say and, in so choosing, made true. This might be the reason my mother left Sri Lanka. In what kind of country would a murder like this happen? Someone killed a man not for being rich or for being powerful—which he was not—but for being respected, which he was.

VAIRAVAN: HE WAS A POSTMASTER. He had spent his life in government service, and in service of those who wrote and those who read. He served all over Ceylon, as it was then known, and when he was sixty-one he retired to a farm in Jaffna with his wife, who like him was known for her great virtue. All of his children and grandchildren lived in Jaffna, or near it, and he dreamed of growing old there, surrounded by them. As a working man, he had learned the value of a disciplined and scheduled life. Even as a retired man, he rose with the dawn and went out to milk the cows.

I think what happened was this: that he woke up one morning and thought that the day would be very sweet and mild, with a sweet breeze. That the sky was just considering becoming light blue, and that the fields looked very ripe and gold, that the rainy season had just passed and the harvest was ripening. I think that he woke up and boiled milk for tea, that he put the leaves of his tea into the pot and brewed it, and that he did all of this without waking his wife. That the aroma of the tea filled the house like a blessing, and that he drank two cups of it before putting his clothes on to go to work.

By the time he went outside, the sky, which was not yet light, was turning from black to dark blue and beginning to forget the stars. This was the best weather for working, because the buildings where the animals were kept could become very hot, too hot at midday for an older man to work. He went down and out into the fields and unlocked the door to the cows' shed. He could hear the cows waking up, and the roosters crowing. And the day was beginning to be sweet, as he had seen it would be, and he was glad that he was still strong and could still work on the farm with his wife. He thought of her, asleep, and he smiled. His hands moved on the body of the first animal, and milk shot hot and foamy into the bucket he had placed on the ground.

When he was done, he took the bucket and went back outside, and the sun had just entered the sky. His figure was the darkest thing about the horizon. He could hear the sounds of his wife stirring inside the house, and he was bringing the milk back to her when he heard what he thought was a loose animal, or perhaps a dog worrying the garden. There was a sound like a heavy step on old leaves. He put the bucket of rich milk down on the grass carefully, so that none of it spilled. He went around the corner of the shed to see what the noise was.

HIS WIFE FOUND HIM lying bloody in the fields.

She had searched for him silently and alone when he had not come back into the house. She had followed his path easily, knowing by Heart the shape of his heavy step in the grass. She had stopped only for a dark moment of clarity when she saw the beginning of a bloody and a beaten path that went into the meadow behind the shed. Whoever had dragged his body had left her a clear trail to track, a path outlined by two red lines that were traceable, she saw now, to his bare and bleeding feet.

His dear face, that she had touched and loved, was cut down to the bone. The side of his scalp had been torn away. His body, that she had touched and loved, was cut from throat to belly in a shallow slit that had been enough to drain him of blood, and this in turn had been enough to kill him. If Murali had been there, perhaps he would have slipped on his gloves and murmured sadly: *I never liked pathology.* Perhaps he would have reassembled the slain man with his doctor's hands that had learned so late to love the body. That was the first test: make the body no one. But this was not Murali. And this was a body that had belonged to someone.

He had been a very handsome man, this great-grandfather, Vairavan. He had had about himself a certain sternness, the same quality that my father would later see in my mother: an unwillingness to relent or compromise that was apparent in his face. Vairavan's children learned to hold this toughness above all else. His look in death still had this quality about it. He had lived a long life, but it was not a life as long as she had wanted it to be. He had not yet become an old man. His wife looked down and with her bare fingers she closed his eyes. She put her hand under his unshaven chin and lifted it. She thought to cry out for someone and then she did not. She looked down at him, her husband, a terrible fury and sorrow fueling in her chest. She had known he would die. Someday. But this was not the body she wanted to remember.

THEY NEVER CONVICTED ANYONE in the murder of Vairavan. He was so loved that no one in their village of Urelu could understand why anyone would kill him. When his daughter, my great-aunt, told me about what had happened, the most descriptive word she could bring herself to say about her father was "respectable." A man who had been like any other, a catalogue of small daily preferences and mannerisms, the kind of habits I collect as I collect people. But "respectable" was all she said.

They tried and acquitted a man. No one in Vairavan's family went to see the trial. What did it matter? No one cared who had killed him. The how: it did not matter. Only this mattered: they had loved their father and he was dead. Death was not yet a malleable commodity. It meant only one thing. This was an introduction to violence, before the government and the Tigers made it a country where death meant many different things.

NO ONE EVER SAID it had to be this way, and yet everyone did it this way: all the choices they made about how they constructed their lives were made because of him, and thinking of him, this man whom they had loved and who had been slain by someone they did not know. And this was a time when murder was still unusual, when disappearances were still unusual, and this was because it was a country in which people thought that the sky was considering turning blue, that the fields were growing full of richness and harvest, that the young men and women would go to school and the British would not be there, and that meant that everything would eventually be all right. That when the British were gone, they might fight one another with words, but that no one would ever be murdered again. They had thought it would become impossible, and instead, it was becoming more possible all the time.

There is a period before war like the scent of the air before a storm: the earthy smell of thunder and the ground beginning to open up, sensing the coming rain. Their father had dreamed that young men would marry and have children, as he had done; that young men would go to work for their country, as he had done. That they would live long lives. And this he had not done, and perhaps this for my mother's family was the beginning of an awareness of the place around them: both the sacredness and the coming disaster.

Perhaps his dying can be marked on the clock as the time when things began to go wrong. And when everything went askew, perhaps they thought of him more, his body lying bloody and loved and alone in that field where he had been killed. Or perhaps because of the kind of man he was, they did not think of him lying in the field, but instead, walking through Urelu, in which he had been very much alive. When they grew up, they saw that they could not be alive for much longer in this country, and so they left.

BUT FIRST THEY WERE MARRIED. With only two exceptions: my mother, Vani, and her aunt, Mayuri. It was through her young aunts, Vairavan's daughters, that Vani first saw Marriage. And it was only much later that she understood it.

Marriage Undone: Mayuri, my mother's aunt, was going to marry a cousin-in-law, Bala. Dr. Balachandran. He was a skinny man, with a face that was a little foolish and younger than his years. He was soft-spoken, well-meaning, bespectacled, and when he began haunting the porch steps in the evenings to talk to her, my mother's young uncles talked among themselves. Over weeks, over months, they watched as this man's presence drew their reclusive sister outside. Mayuri was the most difficult of the Vairavan women; she was smart, but unwilling to soften herself for the sake of social grace. She was difficult, snappish, peevish, waspish. Her siblings wondered why the mild young man wanted to marry her. They were not alone in their suspicion; no one thought their two personalities a logical match. But with each visit Dr. Balachandran paid to the porch steps, their sister's face grew softer and her shrill voice quieter.

The visits went on for so long that the siblings wondered if Bala did intend to ask for Mayuri's hand. He was, after all, a cousin—his visits to the stoop could be merely family interest. But it was Mayuri he sought out, repeatedly. When they heard his step up the stone path to the door, the siblings would scatter across the house, or down into Urelu village. Finally, one day, panic-faced, he went into the house to speak to her father, Vairavan. Her father did not give his consent then but said that he would let the doctor know of his decision. Bala went away expecting to hear quite soon that his Heart's Desire was granted. He knew that some caution was necessary on her father's part. Some dignity had to be granted. It would be Improper to decide too quickly—but he was almost certain. He was a doctor, and doctors were the most sought-after men. Then, as now, Marriage to a Doctor falls into a category of its own. Becoming a doctor in Sri Lanka automatically makes a man many times more desirable. Marrying a doctor was a step up, not just for the young woman involved, but for her entire family. So Bala felt satisfied. He was a shy person, and he had spent weeks working up his courage to speak to her father.

He allowed the summer night to swallow him up again into bachelorhood and darkness. As he disappeared into the evening, he passed once more the girl on the doorstep.

WHEN MAYURI'S BROTHERS AND sisters saw her face they knew that something had changed. Bala had asked to marry her; his wish would be granted. Her brothers exchanged grins. She said nothing. She did not have to. In a village such as Urelu, news travels more than quickly. Neighbors exchanged whispers over fences. Relatives gossiped over cups of tea. Astrologers admitted to being consulted. When word of the Proper and Happy Marriage reached Mr. Thiru, who lived a few houses away, he was unsettled. He was a meddling man. It was too lucky, really, he thought. Such a Lucky Marriage in what was already an inordinately lucky family, with its inordinately good father.

There are no evil intentions in a village as intimate as Urelu. Only evil deeds with good intentions. The young doctor wanted to marry Mayuri. He wanted it, thought Mr. Thiru, somewhat irrationally. Mr. Thiru liked Mayuri. He was a cousin by marriage too. He was happy for her happiness. But Marriage to a Doctor falls into a category of its own. Marrying one of them was a step up, not just for the young woman involved, but for her entire family. Why did Mayuri need to marry a doctor? Some of her family had already married doctors.

Mr. Thiru thought about it—but not for very long. Then he picked up the phone and called his shy young friend, Dr. Balachandran. There was another family he knew, a poorer family, that had a daughter of marriageable age. That family deserved their chance.

THE PORCH VISITS STOPPED. At first Mayuri told herself that Bala must be waiting for her father's formal permission to treat her as the woman he would marry. She sat on the steps, slapping away the mosquitoes that landed on her shoulders, looking into the dusk to see if he would appear, this Man Who Desired Her. Three nights passed. None of them was disturbed by his quiet step.

By the fourth night she knew he would never come again. In the mornings she rose and ate her breakfast. She did not speak. Her brothers and sisters watched her, but they too said nothing. Every day she went to work as though nothing was wrong; every evening, she took her place on the porch with two glasses of lime juice as though nothing were wrong. *He will come,* Mayuri said to herself, even though she knew he would not. One night as she sat out there, she heard her mother, Lakshmi, talking to their neighbor over the back fence. There was a quiet murmur of conversation and then a long pause. Lakshmi came out onto the steps and stood behind her daughter. Then she bent down to put her hand on Mayuri's shoulder.

Mayuri had been teetering on the brink of Mutually Agreeable Arranged Love. Instead, she fell into a chasm of disillusionment, not with life itself, but with the idea of Ever Marrying. She shook her mother's sympathetic hand from her shoulder, got up, and walked into the house.

In a way she never came out again. She never married, and this was not by choice. And Vani saw her do nothing to change her own fate.

YEARS PASSED, AND SO Vairavan was already gone by the time Mayuri's younger sister, my mother's Aunt Harini, found a different problem: Marriage to the Wrong Man. Or was he?

Harini and Rajan had known each other since they were young and had wanted to marry each other for as long as they had known what marriage was. Urelu thought them a bit of an odd couple. Harini, Vairavan's third child, was a good daughter. She was tall and beautiful, with a sturdy, thin frame and big eyes that looked very dark against her fair skin. She was also shy, and intelligent enough to know that her striking face could attract the kind of attention that would embarrass or even endanger her. She did not want people looking at her as they looked at her sisters and the other young women of the village. So Harini perfected the art of Hiding in Public. She learned plainness. She managed to dress her beauty down. People hardly saw her until she was twenty yards ahead of them. She walked with her long lashes dropped over those huge dark eyes. She passed through crowds and a full minute later, they wondered to themselves: *Was a very beautiful girl just here?* And then they shook the thought away, unsure.

Rajan was a tall, thin, rangy youth, cheaply handsome and mustachioed like the hero of a bad movie. People saw him no matter where he stood in the room. They noticed his flashing teeth twenty yards behind them. They liked him and, at the same time, did not like themselves for liking him. He was more than a bit shiftless. He had a set of friends apart from Harini, a wilder clan of young village men whose backgrounds were dubious. They smoked and drank to an extent that any mother would frown upon, but especially Harini's. But she was friends with Rajan's mother, and it was this friendship that allowed her to tolerate the idea that her Harini might end up with Rajan.

Harini had a calming influence on him. Rajan around Harini

was like a different person: quieter, calmer, more like his father. And around him, guarded Harini forgot to let her long hair fall in front of her face. The mask fell away from her beauty. They loved each other so clearly and simply that Lakshmi sighed, remembering when she herself had been so young.

So when Rajan's mother leaned over the bougainvillea one morning and said, Lakshmi, don't you think it's time we talked about the children? Harini's mother did not ask what she meant. Instead she paused, and nodded slowly.

SOMETIMES THIS IS HOW Marriages are Arranged: rather than setting the pattern of love, they follow it. Harini, even bundled in her Wedding-Red, was not the star of the wedding. Nor did she want to be. All eyes were on the groom, who seemed to be swathed in light, a dark-skinned man with coconut-white teeth gleaming in a movie-star smile. Harini's Heart said *thump thump thump* to that smile. Rajan looked at her across the ritual wedding fire and the smile changed to a conspiratorial grin. *I know you,* it said. *I have you.* He had her. But Harini's Heart did not trust that grin. Shut Up, she told it and held her foot out daintily for him to slide the silver wedding rings onto each of her second toes. His fingers on her ankle felt good, and she thought for a moment, irreligiously, unchastely, Improperly, how those fingers might feel in other places. Irritated at herself, she bowed her head so that he could garland her.

The priest droned on in Sanskrit, then in Tamil. She looked up and saw her mother, standing next to Rajan's. Rajan's mother looked beatifically happy. Beside her, her own mother was imposing and impassive. The temple bells rang, and her sisters moved among the wedding-goers, handing out fruitcake. The guests were hungry. This country did not take Marriage lightly: here, getting Married could take all day.

HARINI AT THIRTY: SHE remained painfully beautiful, unnoticed in Rajan's shadow, with a child on each hip. He still attracted attention too, flashing his coconut-sweet movie-star smile with a wild edge at its ends, tucked under the mustache. They walked through crowds, him slightly ahead of her, and Urelu, which had grown used to Rajan but never to Harini, gossiped. She had been the good daughter, the one every mother wanted her son to Marry Happily. How had she ended up with this rake? For this is what Rajan had become—a rake. He did not outgrow the habits of his youth. He drank too much. He fooled around. Sometimes when he came home at night and joined Harini in bed his hair had the sweet pungency of ganja. But Harini never said anything. She smiled serenely, even when he grew belligerent in the market with the fruit vendor, or when he slapped their youngest child at whim. He screamed at her in private, then in public, pulling at her long hair. One day a big clump of it fell into his open palm, and they both stared at it, astonished. Then he hit her across the cheekbone, and Harini's mouth flooded with blood.

This is the taste of a Marriage Dying, her Heart said. Harini had swallowed everything, all her life. Her spinster sister Mayuri's jealousy of a Marriage that had happened too neatly. Her mother's quiet disapproval. Her own self-imposed status as a perpetual shadow. Harini swallowed again, swallowed air and blood. Her beating Heart had grown pulpy and old with abuse.

But Harini bent double, bent down. She picked up her Go-On Forever Smile from where it had fallen on the ground, and went on.

SOME MARRIAGES DO THAT. They go on even when they should not.

Even childhood sweethearts cannot prevent their lives from being twisted into shapes they never expected. Logan, Harini's oldest brother and my mother's favorite uncle, sometimes wished he was not the eldest in the family. With eldest son–ship comes responsibility. It fell to him to say something to Harini about her husband.

The year that Harini's oldest child was seven, the family came to visit Logan's house near the tea estates, where he worked. As Harini walked over the threshold, Logan held the door. His sister's head passed directly beneath his eyes, and he saw for the first time threads of gray in her thick, straight hair. And beyond that, the bare spot behind her left ear.

He looked up to see Rajan behind her on the path to the house, their younger child hoisted carelessly on one shoulder. Logan resisted the urge to reach out and take the child from him. There would be time enough for that. Rajan reached out to shake his hand, and Logan took it. He did not embrace him warmly, as he might have one of his other in-laws. He was a little older now, more austere, his own gray beginning to show above his temples. Logan closed the door behind Rajan. They were now in his house, a house that for years had held nothing but Safe Love. Harini caught herself inhaling deeply, as though she could absorb this through her skin.

Logan's wife, Kala, motioned to the elder of her two daughters from the kitchen. The girl took the tea tray from her, placing the sugar bowl with its precise cubes into its holder. She handed around the tea and passed plates of food, steaming rice and curries. Harini looked up and saw that Kala's daughter was tall and pretty, neatly dressed. Obviously Loved. Harini picked up her teacup and noticed that although she had not seen Kala for a long time, the older woman had remembered without asking how both she and Rajan preferred their tea. She looked up and saw that her brother was much thinner now, that his walk had become more measured. He seemed to her to have found a new easiness within his own body. She saw that her eldest brother had come to remind her of their father, and this made her love him more.

They sat in the parlor and talked for hours. After a while, Kala excused herself and took all four cousins to their beds. She did not return, and after a while, Logan realized why: she did not want to talk to Rajan, who had clearly been drinking heavily earlier that day. The three of them, Harini, Rajan, and Logan, sat there in the parlor until it was very late. Logan wondered if he could outlast his brother-in-law, who had burned a hole in the arm of the settee with a cigarette and not even noticed. It would be improper and perhaps offensive to ask for a moment alone with his sister. Finally, as the short hand of the clock moved toward midnight, Rajan yawned, a fuzzy alcoholic yawn, and excused himself, cocking a brow at his wife, who shook her head timidly. He inclined his head, *good night*, and meandered down the hall to the bed that had been prepared for them.

Logan's eyes followed Rajan out, then returned to his sister, whose beauty had turned stark since he had last seen her. There was a small bruise on her cheek, he noticed, and it looked very slightly swollen. He reached out and put a gentle finger on it. He had been prepared to say something to her about her husband, perhaps a simple and direct conversation that would have gone like this:

You shouldn't stay with Rajan.

She would have looked at him and blinked, her Go-On Forever Smile still fixed on her face.

There's nothing else to do, she would have said.

But they did not have this conversation because it was not required for them to understand each other. Instead, he looked into her eyes and saw her reply. He saw that she was right. He saw that she knew Rajan drank and smoked to excess. He saw that sometimes she did not know where her husband spent his nights. He saw that her husband still hit her, and that she had issued an empty threat to leave him. He saw that she had chosen not to recalculate her own life. Her face had changed from one of hidden beauty. It had become a beauty that constantly consumed itself and was reborn: a phoenix face in its fierceness, its insistence on survival.

Logan got up, walked down the hall to his own bedroom, where his wife the Loved was sleeping, and woke her up.

If you could help her, he said to Kala.

Kala sat up and rubbed her eyes, already knowing what he meant, already having seen the bare spot and the bruise and the place where Harini's Go-On Forever Smile had gone crooked.

FOR TEN YEARS HARINI died that way every day. Then one day she walked out into the garden to find Rajan fallen. She swallowed, and stopped smiling, missing him already.

MY MOTHER KNEW AND LOVED her aunts, but even as a little girl, she chose not to be close to them, because she did not understand their failure to create what they wanted. How Mayuri was left on those porch steps with two glasses of lime juice. How Harini stayed with a man who did wrong and wrong and wrong by her. How had they allowed this? She watched them and took from them Mayuri's persistence, Harini's willingness to smile through pain.

The rest she left, although she loved them. This is how she became the woman who left Sri Lanka, chose my father, and stood against a family that believed in Propriety and Tradition.

AND YET, VANI DID not choose to leave Sri Lanka forever. She chose not to go back. It is not the same thing. But in a way, her reasons were the same as my father's. When the conflict begins must depend, like everything else, on the memory you acquire.

First: Who are you asking? To read the story in the press is to read a story that has never gone far enough. Ask one relative and this is how the story begins: the international Tamil conference came to Sri Lanka, and the government wanted it to be held in Colombo, which was the capital of the country. The Tamil organizers wanted it to be held in Jaffna, the northern city, which was their capital, and so they declined to move it. At the opening of the conference some government soldiers came and shot some young Tamil men. Almost all of them died, and this was what sparked the beginning of the actual violent rebellion: this blatant killing. Whereas before there had been quieter violence or discrimination. Those who attended the conference were mostly young men, young aspiring politicians who grew into old men with old memories of their friends who were killed. If you ask someone else, they will tell you a different story, say that the Tamils were making it all up, that there was no discrimination, that the island was an island of three languages and cultures, and that those cultures were equal before the Tigers began killing people, including their own. Ask another, and another. None of the stories will be absolutely complete, but their tellers will be absolutely certain. This is how we make war.

But there are some things that are indisputable: even now, it is the young men who disappear. The odd foreign journalist, here and there, but mostly the young Tamil men. Fathers fret anxiously over the whereabouts of their sons. Every night, mothers set places at meals for their boys. And every night, in many houses, some of those places go unfilled. There are people whose job it is to collect the names of the absent and to set them down, record them, send them to as many people as possible, humanitarian and political organizations. This hardly ever accomplishes anything. Years later, when children in other countries ask their parents about going home, their parents say no, that's not a good idea, not this year, it will be too expensive.

What they do not say: it is too expensive because the country runs on bribes, because you have to pay the police and the army and probably a professional escort to navigate for you, because the four-star hotels are the ones with the most security, not the greatest amenities, because you can only go home again if they promise not to bomb the airport.

And so, halfway around the world, here I am. Telling you about my mother's family. My mother herself would tell you that it began when she was ten. In the anti-Tamil riots of 1958, when she was visiting Colombo. They were on a road of Tamils, in Wellawatte. But one Sinhalese family lived there too. When they heard the mob coming, they shut their Tamil friends in their house, to wait in the quiet and the cool and the dark for the end. Vani, the little girl who grew up to be the nursery school teacher, Murali's wife, and later my mother, hid under a table. The Sinhalese family passed food through the cracks in the doors and the windows, and the Tamils waited and watched, knowing that it would be over and that it would start again.

I HAVE LEARNED THAT one way to get my mother to talk about herself is to ask her about other people, other things. It is a trick, really, nothing more. She is someone who is faithful to history and so she cannot help but include herself in the narrative as an innocent bystander, a silent guest. In this manner you can extract her character, piece by piece, because even the most self-effacing person can only remain an innocent bystander for so long before conceding to the power of her own past presence.

When Vani was at the convent school in Kandy, studying to be a teacher and beginning to be beautiful, she would often spend her weekends at Logan's tea estate in Nuwara Eliya, which was nearby. She was horribly homesick, and visiting her uncle Logan and aunt Kala made her feel closer to Urelu. Late in her childhood, her uncle had become the superintendent of three tea estates, which made him someone of considerable importance. She remembered his house having a formidable formality. He was a *dorai*, and this meant that he was a man of stature, someone important. A man in charge. His wife, Kala, who was the *doraisāmi*, was similarly intimidating. Logan ran the business of the plantation, and she ran the sizable house. They were both jobs that traditionally required homage to ceremony and to manners. It was not until much later, after both my mother and her uncle had emigrated, that her stories of him managed, finally, to permeate the shield of colonial formality that had been imposed on their lives in that place.

Logan resembled his late father, Vairavan, in many ways, except that the sternness in his face was a bit more sharply drawn. He had a lowering brow and a pronounced jaw. Only the rare and broad smile transformed that imposing face. He was a busy man, and he made time especially for his nieces and nephews when they arrived at his estate on holidays. They arrived by train, and it was a long ride, so when they arrived, they were always very hungry. They were not very old, but they had been taught how to behave, and so no one ever mentioned being hungry until they reached the house and were asked in to dinner. They were met at the station by the *dorai*'s man, who picked them up in a big, broad, black car that belonged to the estate and was at their disposal for the holiday. They clambered into it, always holding hands, brother helping sisters up into the high coach, suitcases rumbling in the back. Sometimes when they arrived it was raining, and then the ride to the estate was bumpier than usual and slightly unpleasant. They shivered from the wet and thought of what waited for them: the *doraisāmi*, smiling one of her smiles-with-teeth (which were reserved for people whom she loved specially), holding for them cups of hot tea with sugar (which is how they all drank it; although my mother does not have a sweet tooth, she would never dream of taking her tea *without* sugar—that was sacrilege).

At the gate, Kala took their umbrellas from them and ushered them into the house. The driver followed with their bags, and she brought them into the palatial front room, where they removed their shoes. They always brought her gifts: cans of fruit from their mother; fresh onions and tomatoes; special homemade sweets. After drinking their cups of tea (which always seemed to them deeper and bigger and more adult than those they had at home) they were ushered from the palatial front parlor into the even more palatial dining room, where they waited for their uncle, then ate their dinner, which had always been especially prepared for the first night of their visit.

They waited at the long, high table for Logan. Each place had a glittering set of dinnerware, but they did not touch anything. They always waited in polite silence until the door creaked and he came in, with his long, swinging gait. He always looked impeccable. How did he look so untroubled by an entire day's work on the hot plantations? He twinkled at them, and they forgot to wonder. He had looked very slightly tired when he walked in, but when he saw them, these children, his whole face lit up. During these years his own children were in England, studying, and his sister's children always made him happy. They greeted him and sat down, and then he rang for the cook.

Logan did not have a cook because he was rich; he had a cook because he was a *dorai* and it was one of the amenities to which a *dorai* was entitled. Even now, when my mother recalls these meals, there is a sound of amazement in her voice. That there could be such food, and so much of it! But even the food was not the best part of this house. They were most fascinated by the wire that ran from the kitchen to the wall to the table, under the table, under where Logan's hand rested as he ate. There was a small button there, and if he pushed it, it called the chef back into the room. The children loved this bell, the extra air of command it gave an already commanding man. As though it were proof that so many people listened to him. Which they did.

LIKE ALMOST EVERY MEMBER of his family, my great-uncle eventually left Sri Lanka. There was nothing else to do, and I think that my mother likes to remember that bell under the dinner table, my great-uncle ringing for his servant, although that makes it sound like it was an imperious thing to do rather than merely the observation of custom. I think that my mother likes to remember this and then to think about how her uncle crossed the ocean, how he left, because the juxtaposition of the two memories proves to my mother that Logan is a brave man. This was what her family did: leave Sri Lanka, one by one, piece by piece. Although they left it until it was nearly too late, it was not something that was hard to do, finally—leaving. It was something they achieved, with that toughness that they had hoarded among themselves. My mother's family turned anger at their situation into a way out of the island.

My great-uncle Logan, still an almost-young man then, left the country after the riots in 1983, that great spate of ethnic violence in which Tamils were more often than not the victims. Young men in particular went missing or were beaten on the streets. He had left his position as a *dorai* when the violence began, and as he looked out his window and saw it beginning to escalate, he began to make phone calls. He called everyone he had known in what he was beginning to think of as his former life. The friends of the *dorai* he had been. He had never abused his position. He had never treated anyone unkindly or unfairly. He hoped now that people would remember this. He hoped now that he would be able to secure what he needed from these friends to leave, and to take his family with him.

Someone called back: Two berths to India, uncle? This was luck, he thought; this truly was luck because these berths were beginning to be almost impossible to get, the ships crowded with the hard quick hurried breath of those escaping. Everyone he had ever known was leaving. He and Kala went over the sea on a ship to India, surrounded by men for whom he had worked and who had worked for him his entire life. They took almost nothing with them: a suitcase apiece. Everything else they left behind. Kala could not even bear to pack up the house. They left it untouched, with the two tall oil lamps from the tea estate shrine still guarding the front door. As though these symbols of prosperity could keep it inside the place in which they had once conducted their lives.

I THINK THAT MY MOTHER was proud to remember what Logan had been like, and that he was able to leave all of this grandeur for a far simpler life. This was what their family did: left Sri Lanka. This was something he did many years later, when my mother was already gone. Later, in Canada, he worked as a security guard for a time. In his adopted country, which was unsafe in new and different ways, it was a job that paid well. This was a profession that many Sri Lankan men took up after leaving their country. At home they might have been bankers, engineers, accountants, *dorais*. In the West, they looked after others, as they had once been looked after themselves.

This is how they left: they took the boat to India, and from there spent most of their money buying plane tickets to England. After a few months in England, they decided to try for Canada, which was taking Sri Lankan refugees. They bought tickets to New York. They did not have any money left for tickets back, and this was a calculation that worked perfectly. They landed in New York, and an acquaintance picked them up and drove them to the Canadian border. There, he left them with nothing. This was not abandonment; this was planned. To show, formally, that you were in need. To demonstrate that you were seeking refuge. And this is something that can still be done with honor.

Leaving: this is how it is done. Logan, who had once been a *dorai* of a tea estate in Sri Lanka and who was now just another Tamil refugee, walked toward the officials at the borders, his hands spread wide and open to show that he had nothing. Like a soldier surrendering, revealing that he is unarmed.

THE OTHERS, TOO, ALL found their way out, one by one, each one proving to my mother that she had been right to marry my father, and that she would be right not to go back. More than anyone else, my aunt Kalyani, my mother's older sister, is a labyrinth of information about these leavings. She keeps within herself the tiniest memories about the lives of those around her. She had once wanted to be a doctor, but when she failed the university entrance exams she became a teacher, and then a mother. She was such a spectacular success at both that almost no one remembers now that she wanted to go into medicine. That she used to sing on All-Ceylon Radio.

Twenty-five years after Vani hid under the table in the 1958 riots, there were riots again in Colombo, where Kalyani had moved. In the riots of 1983 the soldiers burned Kalyani's house. The choreography of her life at that time was very simple.

Kalyani is sewing now as she tells the story, patient and calloused fingers working at the pattern on a sari blouse. Her voice is matter-of-fact.

It all started like this, you know. There are the Tamil Tigers who want to separate the north. The boys in Jaffna set up a land mine, right, which killed thirteen Sri Lankan army officers in Jaffna, *ceriyā? Do you have that?* They were passing in a truck, and the land mine was set off and about thirteen officers died on the spot. They were all Sinhalese. That sparked the riots. It was July 23, 1983. A very hot day. The riots began the next morning. They started burning and looting. Houses were burned down, people were killed. The whole of Colombo was burning.

The twenty-fourth night, a curfew was declared by the government for the next three or four days, but the looting and burning continued. I did not leave the house, and I did not allow my husband or my children to leave the house. Then, on the twenty-fifth night, some thugs brought torches to set our house on fire.

When Kalyani saw the thugs coming down the road, she went to tell her husband, who was in the garden. Together they went to find their children, Haran and Krisha. The four of them jumped over the low wall into the neighboring garden and stayed hidden in that house. The man who owned the house was an atheist from northern India, who had kept himself apart from the conflict surrounding him. From her hiding place Kalyani could hear him talking with his caretakers about his business and the weather. As though there were not a war going on outside. She could not really believe it. There were the sounds of the men pacing back and forth and conversing, and under that, a steady sound of crackling and falling: the sounds of her house burning. She closed her eyes and listened to glass breaking and men yelling, the very calm and even voice of the Indian man speaking to his servants. She thought to herself, *A funny type of man, to argue that there is no God.* Perhaps the gods thought it an amusing jest, to have someone who did not believe in them be the person who saved Kalyani's life. When the riots died down they crept back into their house to see what was left, and found there was nothing but a shell of where they had lived.

When the riots died down, they all went to Haran's school and slept there for weeks, surrounded by other Tamil refugees in a makeshift camp. It was very hot and very crowded and they lay body to body on the floor of the school. Even in their sleep they dreamed of one another's sweat. In August, they were sent to Jaffna, crammed into a cargo ship. All the time, people were so close together that it was easy for government officials to forget individual names. This is how people become indistinct, lose each other. You become part of a crowd. Haran was only one of many young men, and to a stranger's eye, maybe a Westerner's eye, they all looked alike. Kalyani wanted to send him somewhere different, a place where his body would not be blurred into so many others. She did not want him to be one of the young Tamil men who disappeared under suspicion of being a Tiger.

A short while later, Kalyani managed to send Haran to the United States to live with Vani. He was just the right age to join the Tamil militancy, and there was no way he could stay in the country into which he had been born. The following year, Kalyani's husband went to work in the Middle East, and it was just Kalyani and Krisha. Haran never saw his father again; he died in the Middle East. Kalyani herself left Sri Lanka long ago and floats between countries and relatives, a nomad. She is not a permanent part of anyone's life. It is cold here in the United States, too cold for her. It is winter here and it is snowing.

I want to go back to Colombo and live there. I would be on my own. The weather here is not agreeing with me, she says to me now and looks out the window.

Once out of Sri Lanka and into the West, no one goes back. This is unsaid. It would be insanity. Her voice rarely betrays anything selfish, but I am struck by what I recognize in it. *Homesick*. There is nothing to go back to there. Her house was torched. She lived in that house for a decade. My mother has always mourned the burned family photographs, but now I realize how much more was there than just the pictures. My aunt is almost too quiet to hear.

Not only the pictures, she says. Everything. House and property, everything. Nothing left, nothing left.

In a moment, her voice is her own again, matter-of-fact. Her eyes are on the sari blouse, the needle and thread moving in and out of the silk.

THE WEEK BEFORE HARAN left Sri Lanka, a friend of his died. This happened in a way that made Haran wonder if he would ever come back. The man who died was a friend of his, but also a teacher. He was the principal of the secondary school that Haran had attended in Jaffna after the riots. He was a very kind man who had always encouraged Haran to study, despite the hanging despair of their family's displacement. Haran sometimes thought of this man as a grandfather. After he was dead this feeling grew.

The teacher's name was Arun, but his students all called him Sir, even those who had graduated. He inspired in them an absolute and almost British formality. He was already very thin and pale by the time Haran met him, and now, as Haran was going away, he was on the verge of retirement. He had been a teacher for many years. Haran went to say good-bye to him, and to thank him. He did not take anything; he could not offer anything the old man did not have. He felt glad when the door was opened to him to see his teacher's face brighten. This, at least, he could return to Arun—some sort of pleasure in simple company. He liked to think he could make the old gentleman happy in some small way. The two of them sat down in the kitchen, and Arun made Haran a cup of tea without sugar. He did this without asking, and Haran saw by the gesture that the old man remembered him exactly, even to the manner in which he drank his tea. It was a gesture of infinite hospitality and affection that made Haran smile. He had grown up in Colombo, but Jaffna, too, had become a home.

The old man was very excited to see him, and Haran saw that he had some piece of happy news that he had been waiting to tell someone. He thought his teacher still looked well. The old man was a cricket fan and had played for the national team when he was younger. Haran could still see the memory of the strong, sturdy, slim build of the batsman within his teacher's aging, sharper frame. He carried the recollection of his own athleticism, and Haran had admired this vigor in him. He had it even now, at sixty-eight, which was old for a man at this time in Sri Lanka. He was perhaps even dearer to Haran because his very age made real the idea that some people lived long lives. That not everyone died or was ruined in violence.

Arun was glowing now with his news, and Haran leaned over his tea to stir and listen. There was to be a cricket match, the old man explained, a grand match between the students of the school and the Sri Lankan Army team. The old man had arranged it himself, he admitted, and he was looking forward to being the referee. He took out a newspaper to show the announcement to Haran. The item had made the front page. Haran, seeing the notice, smiled wistfully, wishing he could stay to play cricket. The old man saw him sigh and said, There will be other games and other times, young man. Haran smiled and sipped his tea, thinking that he would like to look so well at this age. He thought that he would like to sit with the old man for many more days and nights and hear his stories: about the liberation of Sri Lanka, the great national cricket matches, the tea plantations, the villages at the edge of the sea where men made their living fishing. He thought that no one told a story as well as the old man, and he thought that he would like to be like that, when he was old, if he were ever old.

There is not always another time or another game, not even for the old man whom Haran had learned to love during his short time in Jaffna. After Haran left him that evening, Arun, who had been the master of Haran's school, a gentleman, a scholar, an athlete, was killed. It only took one shot; he did not even know that that was what it was, because the gunman simply leaned through a window and let the weapon touch the old man's skull as he lay sleeping. As though it were only an insect that could be swatted away. Later, they found out that the assassin was a Tamil rebel who was angry with the old gentleman for arranging for a Tamil school to have a match with the Sri Lankan Army.

When he heard the news, Haran's Heart—which had broken with the burning of his Colombo home—broke again. It broke quietly but firmly, and he knew that it could not be fixed this time. He was leaving and that was a decision that could not be retrieved or undone. Now he did not wish for it to be. What a stupid, stupid country, Haran thought angrily. These were the things that ended lives, that ended stories? A cricket match?

AND SO FROM THE TIME she was a child, to well after she left Sri Lanka, my mother knew violence. It went back generations in her family; she had seen it and she knew that it could touch her children, as it had touched her sister's. Because she grew up in Jaffna, my mother fell in love with my father as much for what he was not as she did for what he was. He was not a terrorist. He was not violent. He saw people blown apart and wanted nothing more than to put them back together, just as her brother, Kumaran, had once assembled buildings, in the same manner that she herself constructed minds, gave them a framework. What did she love about my father? She liked the quick, unadulterated sweetness of his smile, which was sometimes so innocent it was like a child's. She liked the way his black hair waved back from his high forehead, that she could see already the honest baldness of his old age. She liked the look of his stethoscope around his neck, and the clean boy-smell of his hands and his neck. She liked that he was young and beginning to go gray; she thought it meant that he had known great sorrow, and that she could relate to that. She knew that if he could have put her brother back together for her, he would have done so. Years later, in a house in Canada, my mother recalled what she thought was her brother's tipping point, the moment when he tumbled across the line of sanity.

He was riding a bus, she said. He was riding a bus and the day was very hot, and so the people on the bus had left the windows open, so as to let in the cool evening breeze. The breeze traveled into his hair and out again. He remembered this very clearly, later, when he was telling us this story, just as I am telling it to you now. I think this is what he intended in relating it, that it be passed on, that things not be forgotten, the way one dead man can be forgotten. It was just a bus, just a bus full of people on the way home, to their mothers and fathers and sons and daughters. But the bus reached a crossroads and a roadblock, and they were pulled over by some members of the army. It was not yet a time of violence, and to be pulled over in this manner was still unusual, and your uncle, my brother, Kumaran, he knew that something was wrong. They all knew, and it blew over them as the breeze had blown over them, and then the soldiers boarded the bus. This made Kumaran very nervous. Just from looking around, he guessed that he was one of the only Tamil men on the bus, and he knew that they had not boarded the bus to search for a Sinhalese man. They were looking for someone, someone very specific. Kumaran looked up and he was horrified, because the soldier at the forefront was aiming his gun directly at Kumaran's head. He gave out a great gasp and began to scream out that he wasn't the person they were looking for, that O God, it wasn't him, but it was too late because the soldier had already fired and the bus was erupting in a panic. Kumaran felt that the side of his head was very sticky and he felt very strange and detached, and he reached up to feel the side of his head. He had been shot at very close range, but he was not dead. How was this? He turned around slowly, his eyes tracking the soldiers more slowly, slower still, because he had been shot and blood was beginning to clog his brain and his vision. And he saw that the soldiers were behind him and that they were handcuffing the man behind him and dragging him away, his bloody shoulder leaving a trail behind him, their footprints in his blood marking the aisle of the bus. He realized that they hadn't been aiming for him, but that if they had been aiming at him, no one would have done anything. He would have died, and he thought about this, and he swallowed, realizing the words that had been on his tongue at the moment that misdirected bullet was fired: O God, it's not me, *I'm not even Tamil.*

He was horrified at what he had almost said. I have always thought that this for him was the second that everything came into focus.

But you can ask him yourself, she said.

[nallu]

DEATH DRAWING NEARER

Those who have been friends and have afterwards forsaken him will return and join themselves to him when the cause of disagreement is taken away.

—TIRUKKURAL, *chapter 53, line 9*

KUMARAN: MY UNCLE, WHOM I LOVED. HE IS DEAD NOW, BUT I remember his body, because in the third month that we were there, my father asked me if I thought I could manage to help him.

I realize that in the Western world, doctors don't care for the members of our families, he said to me. But perhaps you are now realizing that you do not live in an entirely Western world. As a Sri Lankan doctor, I constantly take care of my family. Other Sri Lankans. They ask it of us—they expect it of us.

Us. He was saying us so that I would know that he thought I could do it—be a doctor, like him, putting people back together. Helping whomever I could. Even or perhaps especially someone who was related to me.

Do you think I can do that? I said.

You are not his daughter, he said. I would not ask her to do it, although after what she has been through, she probably could do it. But you *should* do it. It will help him.

I am my father's daughter, and so I began to care for my uncle. As death comes, doctor and patient are more intimate than lovers. I knew everything about his decay, how parts of his body slipped away from him. When he slept, I used to comb his hair gently with my fingers. When the skin at the edge of his scalp started to flake, I rubbed lotion into it. At first, I only prepared food for him; I brought him a wet cloth if he felt warm and made sure that he drank enough water. As the months passed, I knew, I would earn other duties, none of them pleasant, and all of them acts of love: when he could no longer walk, aid to and from the bathroom, and then, the insertion of a catheter, or perhaps a bedpan; when he could no longer ask for painkillers, assessment of if he needed them, and then pills or perhaps injections; when he could no longer eat, the act of feeding him, food or perhaps liquid nutrition. When he became too tired to move, we would turn him over in his bed, plump his pillows, and check for sores. When his fingers became uncertain, when he could no longer turn the page of a book, or write a letter, I would do it for him. When he could no longer speak, I would translate for him. He would tell me: write it down. I told you a story that no one should have to know. Write it down, write it down.

I knew that no doctor should ever have to do this, and I knew that I would do it, because in the end, what he wanted was what anyone wants: to die in the presence of family, with no need for shame or secrets.

VIJENDRAN: A MAN WHOM my uncle did not want near his family. But he was coming back.

After Vijendran and Suthan left on that first day, others started to arrive. They would make furtive phone calls: We hear that someone is staying with you. We would like to come and see him.

Pay our respects, they meant. I did not want them there. I was learning to love my uncle despite what he had done, and they already did, because of what he had done. I heard my mother and my uncle fight about it.

Let them come and see me, he said.

I don't want them here, she said. Don't you think we're being watched? That these conversations are being repeated? Putting yourself in danger—fine, we both know why you're here, that there is limited time. I don't want to fight with you. What about your daughter? What about mine? Do you think that these people coming to see you isn't going to raise suspicion?

I saw my parents confer, late at night. My mother stopped against the wall of the corridor, the small of her back pressed up against it, her head bowed, my father talking at her in a low voice. She had wanted to keep her brother safe; perhaps she had not realized the impossibility of keeping him a secret there, in that closed and yet so open community. It was like a Jaffna village, my father said later: everyone knew everything about him, even before they had seen him lying there in that bed, dying.

Men came, bringing their sons; wives waited respectfully outside the bedroom where he lay. Daughters read books. They did not know him; they had only heard about him. Some of the men, even those who were older than he, called him Anna, which means *respected older brother.* My father thought that some of them left with wallets lightened by my uncle's obligation to the Tigers, his persuasive tongue.

Do you think he is fund-raising here? On his deathbed? Really, Appa?

Well, he said. They let him leave, didn't they? And they have promised his daughter to Suthan, who does the same thing among the boys of his generation.

The same thing? What did that mean? What did Suthan do? The question lay unasked. It followed us around, through the dim hallways of that house, crowded with visitors who told my uncle how grateful they were for what he did, what they did not have to do. Their sons, the right age and size and anger to be militants, in the wrong country. The thing about anger: it always goes somewhere.

KALYANI: MY AUNT ARRIVES in the second month, having left her daughter and her family in Australia to be with her brother during these final days. We go to the airport to get her without him, and she arrives in the same terminal he did. I see the shadows of his earlier self everywhere. When he arrived here, he stood this tall; he could stand, if not for very long. He had hair; he weighed more. He did not know me, and I did not know him. I did not know what he had done, and I did not know what my parents would do for him.

On the ride back, my mother and her sister talk so fast that there are almost no silences between the end of one's sentences and the beginning of the other's. I have seen them together before, but not for many years, and I catch my aunt's eye. She sees me laughing at them and pauses to smile back at me. I love her for this: she will make room for jokes in the worst of situations. We have picked her up to see her brother die, and she knows that some things are still funny—she and my mother foremost among them.

She pauses. Only child, she says to me. You should have had a brother, or better, a sister, and then you would understand.

My father recoils a little and I see this in the rearview mirror, and he does not meet my eyes. I know that my father is glad that I am a girl, that he thinks that this keeps me safe from Suthan's world, and whatever he does there. I already know that he is wrong.

LUCKY: AMONG THE MEN WHO came to see my uncle as he lay there dying was a classmate from his days as a student in Jaffna. Lucky, whose real name is Lakshman, knew my uncle long ago, before he joined the Tigers and before Lakshman's own brother, a politician, was killed by them for daring to disagree with them. For daring to say that they did not speak for all Tamils, that they did not speak for him. That he did not believe in war.

Although I do not have a sibling, I know that one's relatives do not always share one's politics. My uncle has always been the best example of this.

When she opened the door for Lucky, my mother rushed to hug him, and she looked glad to see him. She had not shown that happiness to any other visitors.

I didn't think you would come, my mother said to Lucky, considering.

Considering what? Lucky said, spreading his hands wide. My brother is dead. Yours is alive. That one is alive after all this, we should be grateful.

As Suthan had stood behind his father and loomed, a girl stood behind Lucky and made herself tiny. She was not actually tiny, but she pulled her lanky frame back, holding it close, so that she did not overtake her father. I liked her already for this.

I brought my daughter, Lucky said. She looked so much like him that she could not be anyone else. They shared the same long, straight nose, and the same crinkles at the corners of their eyes. My mother embraced her too, and, awkwardly, she allowed it.

Where is Lalitha? my mother asks.

The face of the nameless daughter shrank a little, miserably, at this question. Lucky's face did the same. I guessed that it was her mother, his wife.

Lalitha could not come, Lucky said.

I brought Rajani, though, Lucky said, his voice too bright. Because I thought, perhaps, your daughter? Would like to go out? They can take the car?

Rajani looked at me, and I looked back at her. We were already friends, united in a desire to protect our parents from this, whatever this was. But as with everything else, we were too late. Decades too late.

RAJANI: I LIKED HER because of her shyness and her bluntness, an odd combination that meant that when she spoke, she always said something that mattered.

Let's go to a little Jaffna store, she said, catching the car keys her father tossed to her. She had not even taken off her shoes. My father said you hadn't seen any of it yet, and that should be enough to entertain anyone. It's like the village. I mean, really. We can get some takeout.

Take-out what?

You can get take-out Sri Lankan food here, she said. I know your uncle wants your mother's cooking, but you can get everything here: fish cutlets, *vadai*, mutton rolls, *dosai*, *pittu*, *idiuppum*, everything.

She was starting her father's station wagon, buckling her seat belt, before I even realized it. I was still standing in the driveway.

Are you coming?

I got in the car and before I fastened my own seat belt, we were off. The roads of Toronto continued to be a maze to me; it all seemed like a big circle. But I recognized the part where we stopped. She pulled into a main drag where it seemed like every parking lot was full of Sri Lankans—women in day saris, coming out of jewelry shops and grocery stores, tugging the hands of small children sticky with Indian sweets. And I saw a steady stream of young men whose dark jeans, sneakers, and close-cropped hair resembled Suthan's.

My father says that your cousin is getting married, Rajani said, parking.

She did not waste time, Rajani. I had to admire that. I had learned the value of this habit myself. No time to waste here.

Yes, I said. To Vijendran's son, Suthan.

Her eyes widened.

Really?

My parents had not told me not to tell anyone.

Yes. Why? What about him? I asked.

Nothing, she said dryly. But if you were not a Sri Lankan and wanted to buy, say, a large shipment of drugs in Toronto, he might be one of the people you could ask. I'm not even sure his father really knows that. But all of us do. The kids, I mean.

You don't seem like the kind of person who would know that, though, I said.

You mean, I seem good? She grinned, and she looked even more like her father, with his pleasant smile.

I laughed. Yes, you seem good.

She shrugged. Should we get out of the car? She opened the door on her side, but then turned around to look back at me.

I am good, she said. Suthan? Suthan is not.

I followed her into the store she had selected, a sari store. A bell rang as we entered. Sari after sari lay in glass cases.

It's good that we're here, then, she said. You'll need a sari for her wedding. She'll need a sari for her wedding.

What do you mean? About Suthan? Rajani?

The women behind the counter were watching us, probably because we were speaking English and did not have any mothers with us. Other young women milled around the store, attended by mothers anxious to ensure their propriety. Rajani and I had no one.

You can call me Rajie, she said.

All right. Rajie. Tell me what you mean about Suthan.

She called to one of the women, beckoning her to our end of the glass counter with a sudden, convenient smile. When the woman came over to us, Rajie spoke in such fluent Tamil that I was shocked. She pointed to one sari, another, another, another.

How do you feel about green?

Yes, green is fine. How do you speak Tamil?

I made myself, she said. That's all. You have to decide to do it. Where you came from, there probably was no option. But here there is school, there is a community. You just have to decide that it matters. Decide to go, to speak to your parents in their language.

She glanced over at me.

I'm sorry—I don't think it means I'm better than you. I mean, a little. She smiled. It's probably far more shocking that I speak Sinhalese, she said. My mother is Sinhalese.

Lalitha, I said.

Yes, she said.

She isn't coming to visit my uncle, I said.

No, she isn't coming.

Why?

She won't visit your uncle because she hates him. She knows that he was friends with my father, and when she heard that he was here, that he was so sick, she was—

I knew that I loved my uncle then, because I did not want to hear what her mother had said. Rajie must have seen that in my face, because she stopped.

I'm sorry, she said. I have a habit of saying things I shouldn't. But my mother not coming—it's not just some simple matter of rudeness. The Tigers killed her father about ten years ago. My grandfather. I never met him.

I'm sorry, I said, a little stiffly. But I meant it.

No, she said. Don't be sorry. We didn't do this, this stupid war, this stupid fighting. They did this. Your uncle, and the Sinhalese politicians. Some of them are even related to me. They disowned her long ago.

The woman had brought the saris over and laid them out on the glass.

Look at the embroidery, the woman said. Very nice.

How much? I asked.

She lifted one price tag at me, and I winced. Several hundred dollars. Even for a nice wedding sari, I knew that my father would think that this was too much.

Your father won't think this is worth the money, Rajie said. But Suthan? Suthan can afford this. Let's go.

Thank you, Amma, she said to the woman behind the counter, who looked disappointed and then began folding the saris. We will come back, Rajie said to her, and her face brightened just a little bit, although Rajie said it with more than a shade of something ominous.

AFTER THAT, I WENT out with Rajie all the time. It was suddenly something that needed to be done, like washing the car, or going to the temple. My mother needed mangoes; my mother needed a certain special kind of bread that could be purchased in one of Scarborough's Little Jaffna stores. My mother needed bananas, she needed rice. She wanted an order of fish cutlets, so that she would not have to fry them herself and waste precious time she could have been spending with my uncle. She wanted curry leaves, and snake gourd, because it was his favorite. And so once or twice a week, after a day of classes at the university, Rajie would come and get me and we would run errands my mother had concocted to get me out of the house. While we did this, Lucky would visit with my uncle. My father liked Lucky, because he kept coming to see my uncle, although his wife would not accompany him. He liked Rajie even more, because like my mother, although he wanted my help, he thought that I should not spend all my time inside that house, waiting for my uncle to die.

The same was true of Janani, but she rarely left the house. On Rajie's third visit, they finally met.

Hello, Rajie said in Tamil to Janani, extending a hand politely. I saw clearly for the first time that Janani was not friendly—it was not just me; she did not like this place or these people or this country, and she did not want Lucky visiting her father. At the same time, when we moved to leave, her eyes followed us with what I thought might have been envy.

Would you like to come with us? Perhaps? Rajie said uncertainly.

If Janani's face had ever moved, if she had ever spoken in a way to give something away, I might have known what that question meant to her. She was eighteen years old, but so much older. She had done all sorts of things that I did not want to ask her about; she was going to be married. She had never been to college, but she had fought in a war, probably held a gun and knew how to assemble and disassemble it.

Yes, she said. I would like to come.

What she really wanted, although I did not see it at the time, was her mother. She wanted her mother in this life, life here in Toronto. It was not Sri Lanka, but it was the next best thing: full of Tamil people, as close to Tamil country as most of us might ever get. And she wanted her mother to see it with her. Her mother to go to stores with her, to shop and plan for her wedding in a city with no curfew and no bombs. No shelled houses full of holes, no weapons training. She wanted a mother who had never fought in a war. She did not want rebel parents, and she did not want to be a rebel herself. Who really wanted this, after all? Not even Janani, with the fierceness of her belief. Because Janani's mother was not there with us, and Janani could go and buy her Wedding Sari with us, but it would not be the same.

My mother heard us from where she had been doing dishes.

Why don't we all go, she said, coming forward, drying her hands.

Janani met her eyes, and that was the first time I had seen anything there approaching kindness, or gratitude. Not her mother, but a mother, still.

Someone should stay with Appa, she said. We'll go.

JANANI, YALINI, RAJIE: THREE girls together in a sari shop, in a grocery store, in a jewelry store, looking at the kinds of wedding chains available. Janani looked at the spread of materials, the richness of the gold, with hungry eyes, and then looked away, as though she were ashamed. I saw it, but it was Rajie who said:

So, Yalini tells me that you're getting married. Do you have a place yet?

It will be at least a year from now, Janani said.

You need to plan in advance. Why don't we go and see some of the places where you could get married?

We got back in the car and drove around in that big circle. I sat in the back so that Janani, who had a much better sense of direction, could see where we were going. When Rajie pulled off the highway this time, we entered a winding road and then went to a quiet neighborhood, where Tamil children were playing on the streets.

You could go for a long time here without seeing a white person, I said, almost to myself.

Rajie turned around and grinned at me and then turned back to Janani.

That place there, she pointed, is the Tamil community center that your fiancé supports. People get married there. You could get married there.

Can we go inside?

We walked up the sidewalk to the big hall, which was empty. There were new, fake-looking wooden floorboards, and a small stage. I could imagine how it would all fit there. How Janani would be Married to this man, Suthan, and his politics. And how a few decades earlier, my father had walked into a similar hall with his friends and built, from scratch, the altar in which he would Marry Vani. Not yet my mother.

[anju]

KUMARAN WHO STOOD BETWEEN THEM

Although the elephant has a large body, and a sharp tusk, yet it fears the attack of the tigers.

—TIRUKKURAL, *chapter 60, line 9*

CONFLICT WAS ALL AROUND VANI, WHO WAS NOT YET MY mother. It began with her brother Kumaran, the sibling to whom she was closest. He was the second of the three children. In the early 1970s he had gone to England for a brief time. He was in the midst of studying for his engineering degree. He was a very good student, very quiet and serious, with a habit of smiling and then stopping himself from smiling. He went to England a quiet person and came back an even more quiet person, and everyone saw that something in him had changed. He had met someone. Perhaps it was a lover? They wondered. A girl he wanted to marry? This was not the case: Kumaran was in love, but he was in love with a cause, and with the rhetoric of a person who spoke for a cause. In England he had met the founder of the Tamil New Tigers, Victor Rajadurai. Kumaran's family had hoped that he would find a job in England, perhaps stay there and finish his engineering degree, perhaps even sponsor the rest of them to leave. But Kumaran, who had left, came back. This was something none of the rest of them had done or would do: he had purposely chosen to stay in Sri Lanka, although he knew his situation was not going to improve. In 1975 when the mayor of Jaffna was killed everyone in the family was stunned silent, and Kumaran, who was normally silent, went to his room and closed the door, lay down on his reed mat on the floor and stared at the ceiling. No one thought anything of it. Kumaran already knew or suspected who was behind what had happened, and he was not sure how he felt about it.

In England he had met other young men like himself, who had come to England wanting to study and then return to Sri Lanka. They were all uncertain now that this would be a good life for them, and yet it truly did not occur to Kumaran that he might stay in England. To him that would have been defeat. He had been born in Sri Lanka, and he wanted to die in Sri Lanka, in Urelu, where his mother was, and where he thought the mother of his children would probably be. But he had learned to love London too—Sri Lankan London, Tamil London. Young men with long hair read socialist philosophy and talked to one another about how to make change at home. As though—like my father's tea leaves—it could be wrapped in brown paper and taken through the airport. Sometimes mornings found them asleep at a university library, or in the basement of someone's flat, cigarettes burned down to the tiniest stubs after discussing the state of their faraway nation.

And he did go back to Sri Lanka. He was still a young and unmarried man when the rebellion began over the shooting deaths of the Tamil men at the Jaffna conference. There were riots again, as there had been when my mother was ten, and although she did not say so to her family, she thought that she would like to leave, at least for a little while. Until the country became quiet again. Her contract to teach in the United States was for two years and she thought that after that she could come home again. After that, she thought, the climate in Sri Lanka would be better. She could return home and be Married. She could grow old here.

As my mother was preparing to leave, her brother, Kumaran, was preparing to stay. He was still an engineering student in Jaffna, and he had watched his friends die next to him on the streets of his city, and they had been slain by soldiers who belonged to his government. He was a student, a very young man, and this meant that he was revolution-ripe. About to vanish.

KUMARAN: HE WAS A STUDENT. He had grown into a skinny and tall boy with glasses, black rectangles with rounded edges that clung to his nose and framed his narrow-planed, sharp face. He did not look like a man who could go to war, and this was what made him perfect for it. He did not look like someone who would fight, and this was what made him want to do so. He was part of the beginning of the rebellion that grew into the Liberation Tigers of Tamil Eelam. By the time the busful of relatives came to kiss Vani good-bye, he was no longer on the bus. She left, anyway. There are certain tickets you cannot buy twice, because the price is too high. So she did not say good-bye to Kumaran, because he was not there to hear her say it.

Kumaran: he later became very famous in certain circles, but only in an anonymous way: the press accounts rarely—if ever—named him, although his family recognized him from some descriptions, and there was some mention of him in most stories. Vani began to read about him as though he were a stranger, in the newspapers, which never told the whole story of how the Tamil New Tigers turned into the Liberation Tigers of Tamil Eelam, a separatist movement in the northern part of the country where my parents grew up. My parents have never condoned violence as it is practiced by the LTTE. Sri Lankan Tamils are not a violent people; they are a people who have had violence imposed upon them. This is what my aunt, Kalyani, says.

Imagine that you are in a room, and there are ten cats and one large dog. They are fighting. Who will win?

The dog, of course.

She nods: right, right.

The cats are smaller. Of course in the end they will lose. They will die. But they will do everything they can to hurt the dog before they are killed. They will do as much damage as possible. This is what the Tigers are doing.

This doesn't mean that what they are doing is right. But it's easy for someone to look at what is happening and say that in the same situation, they wouldn't do the same thing. Who knows what they would do in such a situation?

And perhaps this is why my family removed itself from the situation. Something even opened a pathway out for Kumaran. But first: his way in.

KUMARAN REALLY DISAPPEARED FOR the first time in what would have been spring of 1976. It was not the spring of 1976, because Sri Lanka does not know what spring is. At first no one realized he was gone. His mother thought he was at university. The university thought he was ill and had gone home for the term. But he was in neither of those places. Kumaran became someone who was defined mostly by what he was not. Now, at this time, by where he was not.

In England, or France, or Canada, or the United States, it would have been spring, but for the members of Vani's family who were still in Ceylon it was summer, because in Ceylon—which was what the British had named it, and something they sometimes slipped and called it still—it is always summer. Kumaran was gone and no one realized this until one day his mother asked everyone at dinner: When did you last hear from Kumaran?

They were all silent, thinking.

Because, she said, he hasn't called me in about a week, and he always calls. You know Kumaran.

But none of them did. Except Vani, and she was already gone.

KUMARAN: IN THE NOT-SPRING of 1976 when he went missing he was very tall, rangy, and fair-skinned. He was not handsome, but he was attractive, and he looked like his father, and he carried himself like his father. He walked with the memory of his murdered grandfather. He had long brows that very nearly met in the middle, and although he always looked angry he generally was not. Rather, he was thoughtful and deliberate, always speaking slowly. Although his hair was black, like everyone else in his family he went gray young, and so his eyebrows were darker than his hair. He would have looked almost entirely severe, except that his ears stuck out slightly. He was still a boy, even if he did not look like one.

His face had once been round but by this time he had lost that particular sign of youth. His face was narrow and thin and getting thinner. He did not have high cheekbones, like the ones Vani had under her young plumpness, but his cheeks were more hollows than cheeks, and this made his face look like a sculpture beginning to erode. He was composed of exceptions. One: his mouth was very thin and ungenerous, except when he smiled. He was older than my mother. What no one realized: he was dying anyway. Any way.

KUMARAN: OVER THE YEARS his face became more ferocious. As he himself became more ferociously loved and hated. He was a civil engineer by training, something that he chose and that chose him. He loved to assemble things and for pleasure would piece together any physical puzzle or machine. His mind parsed each place into possibilities instantly.

He wanted his job to be real. How could a man tell others how to build if he had not done it himself? On his summer holiday before his final year at university for his engineering degree, he took a construction job at a site in Trincomalee. It was the first time he had done such work, and he was not a very big man. The others on the site were mostly men who worked on construction for a living. They were undaunted by the heavy loads, the wheelbarrows full of concrete and the carts full of bricks. They quarried stone and did not quail. He admired them silently, because they were not the sort of men you admired aloud. They were taller than he, and more muscular. They watched him, to see if he could keep up. He was determined to keep up. Each man had an allotted share to do every day; if he did not finish his he would stay far into the night to do so, rather than carrying the remainder of the work over to the next day. The men would leave one by one, watching him. He knew he was being measured to see if he was wanting. Every night he stayed on the site until he had finished his work. He often returned to his hostel in the slow hours of the morning and left again before anyone else awoke. The hostess always left a generous plate of rice for him on the table, and he ate alone every night and every morning and returned to work.

He was fascinated to watch himself change over the course of a season. As though he could go outside himself to admire the vanity of a consciously spare life. He had arrived a thin and rangy man, tall enough but not sturdy. Now his body was acquiring the muscle of a laborer, like those workers whom first the Tamils themselves and then the British had disdainfully called *coolies.* This was a word that to most people still connoted a lower caste, a smaller way of living, a lesser humanity. A class system that some people deny ever existed in Sri Lanka. But to Kumaran, his *coolie* body now became a badge of honor, as he worked among these men who were called by this name. He had always been a student and had looked like a student. Now the midday sun had made him dark, and he was stronger. He had never looked like this, and he observed with a dispassionate interest the change in the way he was treated by passersby. They thought he was something he was not; they thought he was of a lower class. And Kumaran learned to hate not only what the British had done to his country, but what his people had done to themselves.

THEY WERE BUILDING A SHORT wall of differently shaped rocks. The stones were very heavy. This is how he met his Tiger contact: one night, he was staying very late to finish his work. It was hot, even though the sun had gone down; he was working in a *caram*, what the English would call a sarong, and he was perspiring heavily. As usual, one by one the other men completed their work and left to go home to their families. Kumaran wiped his face on his shoulder and thought about the plate of rice waiting for him, the book of Tamil history he was reading, which had been sent to him by his friend Victor. He was just beginning to set another row of stones when he felt a gentle touch, like that of a cat, on his shoulder.

The man who had touched his shoulder was a dark-faced fellow, with a mustache and a white, white smile. His eyes were dark and soft, like velvet. His hair and face were damp from the day's exertions. He handed Kumaran a dipper of water.

Aday, he said. You never finish your work on time.

Kumaran took the dipper of water from him and drank half of it, pouring the other half on his head. It dripped down his neck, down his back, splashing the other man. Sorry, sorry, Kumaran said.

He grinned. That's all right.

Kumaran studied him, this solitary cat's face with its secretive eyes. He had not seen such an easy grin in many months. He already knew who this man was. I finish my work on time, he said finally. I stay here to finish my work on time. I haven't learned how to fit the stones together as well as the rest of you.

What is your name, scholar?

Kumaran.

I am Nadarajan. I will show you how to fit the stones. It is a matter of instinct.

His name was not Nadarajan, Kumaran knew instinctively.

He looked very much like a man his friend Victor had described in a letter, and this was the sort of man who would hide in plain sight, disguise himself, lie coolly. He took the trowel from Kumaran's hand and dipped it into the mortar, spreading a thick line on top of Kumaran's last row of uneven stones with a quick, efficient motion. Kumaran watched him set the row, leaving a small space in between each stone. He seemed to instinctively select the piece that would fit best in each space. When he lay down the next line of mortar, it sloshed into the gaps, sealing the wall. He did all of this in about half the time it took Kumaran to set the same number of stones. He handed the trowel back to Kumaran with a gesture: you do it. Kumaran set the next row, leaving a gap in between each pair. For the first time, each stone seemed to slip easily into place. Then he laid down the next line of mortar. He did this all as swiftly as the other man had done. The man who called himself Nadarajan—at least that day—saw the ease with which Kumaran had learned the new motion and made it part of his thinking. He saw the deceptive strength of Kumaran.

Where are you staying, scholar? At a hostel, no? All right, then, you can come for a meal with me.

KUMARAN BEGAN AS SOMEONE who planned to put places together, and he became someone who planned to blow places apart. After the conference at which some of his young Tamil friends died, Nadarajan began to gather around him a group of men to fight the government. When he met Victor Rajadurai, who had started a group in England, the Tamil Tigers were born. Their goal: the restoration of the northern Tamil homeland as they thought it had been before the British came. No more discrimination or negotiation with a government they saw as infinitely corrupted and corruptible. Their scholar-negotiator: Victor. Their motivator and military tactician: Nadarajan. Someone who was going to fight, anyway. Someone who gathered the most promising people around him without any kind of discrimination, even the kinds that are considered moral. Women. Children. People are the only real weapons. You tied yourself to dynamite, you swallowed cyanide, you hurled yourself into buildings and onto cars. These were honors. Before the battlefield the most elite—young Tamils who believed their chances for a future were dying—ate their final meals with Nadarajan. Later, my aunt would compare the situation to a dog backing a group of cats into a corner. This interpretation of Nadarajan makes him out to be a man who always thought that he was going to lose and did not care.

I have read about Nadarajan, and I no longer believe this to be true. I think that he always thought that he was going to win. Now, some twenty years after he first began striking against the Sri Lankan government, he is named among the most prominent international terrorists. Wanted (glamorously?) by Interpol. Al Qaeda learned its methods from Nadarajan, people say, and there is a curious and bitter fascination in this: there was a war, and it killed over sixty thousand people, and no one stopped to notice. No one even knows if that number is right. And now no one stops to ask why. A country with no oil. A country full of people who were Of Color. A country from which my mother had moved away. She began to miss it before the busful of relatives had even pulled away. My mother and her brother, Kumaran, whom she loved even more strongly than other members of her family, moving as far apart as people connected by blood can go.

Kumaran fell in love with everything that Victor represented. He had already begun to think about the issues of class in Sri Lanka, but all his life he had recognized the lack of parity for Tamils in this country. What is terrorism? Many Tamils do not think the Tamil Tigers are terrorists; just as many, who have had money extorted from them, hate the Tigers. What is self-defense? What of the slow invasion of life in the northern part of the island? Their lives began to disappear, slowly, drained from them, like an insect burrowing inside a mango. We are taught that some things are sacred, some things are never done, some conventions of war must be observed. I think that the Tigers thought of themselves as a private army, the army of a people without a nation, that perhaps they thought of themselves like the Japanese kamikaze pilots of World War II, who flew suicide missions and knew that that was what they were.

Nadarajan: I can tell you about him, although I have never met him. There are sentences about the war in news stories, things that are true and not precisely true. It was a war that my parents passed on to me in small ways: newsletters in the mail with updates, letters from home. A strange inheritance, this grand play in which Nadarajan is the chorus. He is banned in many countries—most countries. Interpol says that he speaks English, but I imagine that he does not want to, because he is fighting a war for the people and language to which he was born.

"Very alert, known to use disguise and capable of handling sophisticated weaponry and explosives, hair combed back, stout build." This is the Interpol description. Above the description

("Person may be dangerous") there are two pictures of him. He has a mustache and, after what seems to me the curious fashion of South Asian men, he has what the Western world would consider too much hair. The lush sign of a fierce and pulsing life. He is forty-eight years old, and this means that he is of the generation of my parents. This means that if what they write is true, that in 1975 he killed the man who was the mayor of Jaffna, he was only a boy. Only a decade younger than my father. Not even as old as I am now. He looks like men whom I have known all my life.

He is not the person who started the movement of the Tamil Tigers. The literature of terrorism (and there is a literature) says that the Tigers began in England. They credit Victor Rajadurai, intellectual revolutionary, Kumaran's London acquaintance. But it was Nadarajan who rose to eminence as the political and military mastermind behind the war that destroyed the country. I have read my father's books. A scholar wrote:* "It is certain that the Tigers would not have lasted so long and been able to inflict so many losses on their enemy if it were not for their fanaticism. Assistance from the Tamil state in India, as well as the Sri Lankan Tamil diaspora from Norway to Botswana, has played an important role. But this, again, does not fully explain the riddle . . . in the final analysis, there is no satisfactory explanation for the Tamil Tigers and their fanaticism."

But there is an explanation: It is Nadarajan. It is Victor. Their sheer charisma and magnetism and capacity for violence. Nadarajan became the face of the movement, but it was Victor who pulled Kumaran in, made him his protégé. It was Victor who was the diplomatic face of the Tamil rebels. It was Victor who let Kumaran go.

* Walter Lacqueur, *The New Terrorism* (New York: Oxford University Press, 1999), p. 196. Quote altered slightly for clarity (explanation of Tamil Nadu).

AFTER KUMARAN DISAPPEARED, my mother did not see him for years. No one in the family did. This ate at her daily. All of them. Then one day one of them—it was Kalyani—saw him on the news and stopped, speechless, breathless, unable even to point and to say: Kumaran. There he is, our boy who is no longer a boy, our boy who has become something that the newspapers would say is barely human.

His mother had known that he was not dead. She felt his chest rise and fall somewhere on the island. But they stopped saying his name, knowing that if they said it aloud, someone far away in the government might hear it, and then they would all disappear. People who had been tasted by a passing wind and spat out again.

KUMARAN WAS THE ONLY one who did not leave, and because he did not leave Sri Lanka he left the family instead. They held and reflected his presence between them, all of them. They wondered if they would even know if he was dead, and for whose deaths he was responsible. People they knew were found in pieces; the conflict and the movement were notable for how many Tamil lives they cost. The first to be killed were Tamil opponents of the movement. *The traitors within.* Once they read a newspaper account of him shooting an injured friend in the forehead to prevent his capture by the Sri Lankan Army. Once they were mailed an unmarked envelope containing the shards of a glass capsule, of the kind that was used to hold cyanide, and took it to mean that he had killed himself and had it sent to them as a message. But then later again they heard stories of him. Letters were slipped under their doorsteps. Like other Tamil families, they paid a Tiger collector who came to their house, asking for funds. They did not ask him about Kumaran. They gave him every rupee they had in the house. His mother thought about the girl they had found for him, the young woman he had planned to marry.

Unfinished Marriage, Promised Marriage: Her name was Meenakshi, and she was a lovely young schoolteacher whose face had begun to look old the day he disappeared. He never wrote to her or called her. There was no contact. They had been friends from childhood, and Kumaran's mother knew her mother. They never talked about where he had gone. One day the women saw each other at the market, and Meenakshi's mother stopped Kumaran's with a light touch on her arm. Meenakshi is going to Australia at the end of the month, she told her. Kumaran's mother knew what this meant, although it was not explicitly stated. She nodded and murmured her congratulations.

But later that month, before leaving on her planned trip to

Australia, Meenakshi was killed by a Tiger suicide bomber in Colombo. Collateral damage. Kumaran heard the news and tried to kill himself. It was only the voice of Victor that stopped him. This is what it costs, my friend, he said.

And Kumaran believed him.

Later, when he fell in Love again, he remembered her. He married Janani's mother in a Hindu ceremony run in the heart of Tiger country, and as he went around the *homām* with her, he watched her feet move in small, sari-bound steps. Tomorrow, and the next day, and the day after, those legs would wear a soldier's uniform. He did not know then that she too would die. He would have married her even if he knew, of course. And she left him with a daughter. A widower, someone who had Loved a Wife—but a Tiger, still.

SUTHAN: HOW IS SOMEONE a Tiger in the new world? On the streets of Toronto, we took Janani shopping, and when we went into a store and told them whom she was marrying, the younger women in particular wore looks of respect or alarm. Janani seemed not to notice.

Between one store and the next, Rajie asked her:

Do you know what your fiancé does?

He works for his father at the car dealership, Janani said.

Right, Rajie said. And he is involved in some illegal activity, so that the money can go back to the Tigers.

What? Janani said, suddenly sitting up and leaning forward from where she sat in the backseat.

No one else is going to tell you, Rajie said. Maybe none of them knows.

It sounds like he is just doing what has to be done.

This whole conversation was in Tamil. I cannot tell you how I understood all of these words in Tamil. Some of them I had never heard before. But it was the clearest conversation. I could not participate in it. This was between them.

What does he do? Janani asked.

I don't know all of it, Rajie said. But a lot of the young men here do it. They say that they believe in the war that you were fighting over there, and they steal, they sell, they deal.

Deal?

Rajie didn't answer that.

Do you know about this? Janani turned to me.

This doesn't happen in the United States, I said, putting up my hands. I don't know anything about this. Suthan is someone the Tigers chose for you. And you let them.

She stared straight ahead, into the bare stretch of highway ahead of us, through Rajie's spattered windshield.

I did things I did not want to do, she said, to reach an end that I thought was just. Maybe he is just doing the same thing. Doing what he thinks he has to do. They would not send me into something I could not do. This is something that is good—for me, for him, for them.

Maybe, Rajie said. Be careful—people who deal in businesses like that have enemies.

SUTHAN: I DID NOT REALIZE that Rajie had known him, growing up, until they encountered each other one day on the driveway in front of our Toronto house.

Rajani, he said, very formally.

Suthan! she exclaimed. Somehow he had surprised her, although she knew that he came around every once in a rare while with his father.

He looked at her, and she looked actually a little afraid.

It's nice to see you? she said, sounding like her father on that first day when he had proposed that we be friends.

Yes, Suthan said. How is your father? Is he here?

He's inside, with uncle, Rajie said.

Vijendran got out of the car and stood up and frowned at her.

Hi, uncle. Well, she said to me, let's go.

What was that all about? I said, walking quickly to keep up with her.

We don't get along, really, she said, almost under her breath.

The reasons were obvious.

He's going to get himself in trouble, she said. It's one thing to support them, the Tigers. Here that's not illegal. But I've heard a story about another man, around his age, who is also running some illicit businesses. And like Suthan, he says he is giving the Tigers the profits. But not all of these men are honest, and if he and Suthan find themselves at odds? Men in war will do anything. In Sri Lanka, some of the Tigers killed other Tamils who disagreed with them. Like my father's brother.

I would hate to see that happen here, she said. In war there are two kinds of people: the people who lose, and the people who profit. The people who make the money, and the people who are driven out. Do you know how many displaced people there are? And then you think that the only way out is to leave, but the war just moves with you. I wish that if people were going to fight here, they would fight to leave it behind.

Maybe that's not so easy, I said, hurrying to keep up with her. Or even right. To just forget it?

I don't know, she said. Ask my father. Ask yours. Ask them whom they Love, whom they trust. If there's anyone left.

[āru]

MURALI

EDGING EVER CLOSER

A crow will overcome an owl in the daytime;
the king who would conquer his enemy must have a suitable time.

—TIRUKKURAL, *chapter 95, line 8*

THE VILLAGE OF ARIYALAI HAS BEEN EVACUATED MANY TIMES since my father left it. War comes and civilians leave—for schools, churches, shelters, emigration. But Ariyalai's citizens still recognize one another across crowds in other countries. Once upon a time in Ariyalai, everyone was related closely enough to be kin, but distantly enough to be lovers. The bloodlines, like the roads, went largely unnamed. It had never been necessary before. But now we follow those attachments with desperation, as though in losing them we might lose track of who we are.

MY FATHER CAME FROM A family that loves without hesitation or embarrassment. Later some of them would grow out of this, but it was in this mood of absolute freedom and passion that they were Married. I told you of Jegan, who spotted Tharshi and asked for her hand when she was twelve. Perhaps their union passed this kind of abandon to their children at birth. My father's oldest brother, Neelan, carried it beyond Jaffna and became to Murali an example of Marriage Done Right—although there were others who cursed Neelan silently and said that he had Married the Enemy.

My uncle, Neelan, the eldest of Tharshi's children, is nearly two decades older than my father, and much loved. If Neelan is not scandalous, then he is at least Out of the Ordinary. Marriage Without Consent was perhaps easier for my father, because his brother Neelan had already Married the Enemy. She was the Enemy only by an ethnic definition. These definitions are always ugly: Sinhalese intruder in a Tamil family.

WHEN HE WAS TWENTY-THREE and a first-year student in medical school—another doctor-to-be—Neelan caught typhoid. No one knew from whom: it could have been another doctor, a patient, a nurse. He was severely ill for nearly three months. He boarded in a private house—across the road from a relative of his future wife. There was no treatment for the fever. One morning, he woke up and found that the men who slept on either side of him had died during the night. He himself was so ill that his mother, Tharshi, thought that even if he recovered, he would have to give up medicine.

During the illness he became friends with his future wife's sister. That was how they met. The object of his affections was only sixteen or seventeen, shy and slight. She was also unusual: Nirosha was a Sinhalese girl from Galle, in the southern part of the island, but she had already traveled to the Tamil north—a rarity in those days. When her parents found out what was going on, they took her back to the south. But after he got better, he could not forget her. He had already been promised to a cousin, in the silent, expected way aunts and uncles had of trading cousins in certain families. But he wrote Nirosha love letters in which their languages were mixed. And eventually, by scraping together their own money, she found her way back to him. After Jegan died, and Neelan took his ashes to the sea, he settled his family's debts. Then he turned to his mother and said,

And what should I do about this girl?

He and Tharshi had never spoken of it, but he knew she knew. Tharshi looked at her eldest son, her eyes full of love and grief. He hoped his own wife always—and never—looked like that for him.

Marry her, Tharshi said.

They were married in a lengthy Hindu ceremony of which her Buddhist parents remained happily unaware. Later a Buddhist priest made peace between the families, and Nirosha's parents forgave her. But when she began visiting around Ariyalai for the first time as his bride, she was welcomed at one house, he remembers, with tea in a broken cup—a small but unspeakable rudeness in a country where all hospitality and love begins with tea.

By 1983, they too lived in Colombo. When the Sinhalese-Tamil riots started, His Wife the Enemy, the Loved, kept him prisoner in the house for a year, afraid for his life. Today everyone has learned how to say *I am not a Tamil Tiger*—in three languages. Neelan and Nirosha are no exception.

LIKE LOGAN, NEELAN WAS the eldest son. He had seven siblings, and six of them did not worry him. The seventh was Uma.

Uma: she was the youngest of his sisters. Slight and frail, she was deliberately quiet rather than shy. She had too-big eyes in a too-small face. They were unusually light in color, nearly amber. They were very clear, still, and distant, like a cool lake into which a stone had never been thrown. As her now-grown sisters had before her, Uma went to school every day at St. Anne's, where all the subjects were taught in English. Every day she walked alone up the hill into the heart of Ariyalai. Every afternoon when school was over, she did not linger to play or talk with the other children, or even to run errands for Tharshi. Uma came home, and went into her room, and closed the door. No one really knew what went on in that room, or in that head. No one was close to her. She was somehow unknowable. Those were not Sri Lankan eyes; they were always elsewhere. In other countries.

Uma was a brain, that much was certain; like Tharshi, she excelled in school. Everyone knew. People whispered to each other about how smart Uma was, how she was always closeted in her room. Now that there were so few children left, it was her own room, and Tharshi did not want to disturb her. But it worried her that the door was never open. She had the uncomfortable feeling that her last daughter was a genius. Not just smart, like Tharshi or Kunju. They had been intriguing, even alluring in their own ways. But Uma was a full-blown genius. And that could be intimidating. What good could genius do a girl? Especially a reclusive girl like Uma? Tharshi was proud of the possibility of genius, egged it on, cuddled it close in secret—but she was a little frightened of her daughter who seemed always to be looking into another country. In the middle of her family, Uma lived alone. Uma was present and absent from the household at the same time. She had no part in the daily fabric of the household as Tharshi ran it. Once inside her room, Uma would not leave even for dinner. Tharshi left trays outside her door. In the morning, she collected the empty plates that had piled up during the night.

EYES THAT SEE INTO other countries come with ears that hear foreign voices. One Sunday morning, Tharshi was sifting flour on the front porch and heard an unearthly cry.

What was that? Murali asked, sitting up. He had been lying in the sunlight on the porch, immersed in a textbook. Tharshi was already running into the house. Murali followed her. She called out for Uma, and there was no answer. She called again, and again, and then for the neighbor.

From the garden came the neighbor's voice: What is it?

Probably nothing, Tharshi thought and did not reply, suddenly feeling sick. She walked down the hall to Uma's room. The door was closed. She knocked hesitantly. There was no answer. She opened the door slowly. Uma was convulsing, her eyes wide open, her mouth moving soundlessly, her hands clamped over her ears, as though the house was full of a sound far too loud to bear.

THE DOCTORS TOLD THARSHI that Uma was probably epileptic. Tharshi called her eldest son to see what he thought. Neelan's pause on the other end of the line was too long, and she knew it, and he knew that she knew it. It was very late to diagnose epilepsy, he told her. It was not a sickness that manifested itself suddenly at sixteen. What was going on in Uma's life? How was she doing in school? Did she have any friends?

Tharshi was even more terrified to realize she knew the answers to none of these questions.

NO MORE WAS SAID OF IT, but as usual, rumor wormed its way around Ariyalai—a place where everyone was related closely enough to be kin and distantly enough to be lovers—and everyone tiptoed around Uma. Neelan called once a week to talk to her. How are you, he asked her. He meant it kindly, but it was a sign of something serious all the same. She always managed to answer without providing any information at all. He had Tharshi take her to an Ariyalai doctor. Uma submitted without argument to being examined, but the doctor diagnosed nothing. Tharshi bowed her head at his answer and did not believe him.

Tharshi met privately with all of Uma's teachers, who told her that her Beloved Fatherless Girl was nothing short of brilliant. Tharshi thanked them. And then she asked: Has she been acting odd at all? How does she behave in class? Does she have any friends? It embarrassed her to be so vocal and persistent. She was accustomed to asking for little. The teachers looked at her with curious eyes but answered her politely. Some of them had gone to school with Tharshi themselves. They pitied her, playing detective in her own daughter's brain. Tharshi felt their pity, resented it, put her resentment away, and waited patiently for them to tell her what was wrong with her daughter, her precious Uma, with her too-big eyes in her too-small face. Those luminous eyes that saw into other countries. Otherworld eyes. In the end what they were able to tell her amounted only to this: *Uma has always been odd.*

Tharshi thanked them for telling her what she had already known.

IT HAPPENED AGAIN ONE day on the way home from school. One of her older sisters had lent Uma a bicycle, a rare favor, so that she could transport a very large project to school. As Uma rode home with her basket full of books, her hair, which had grown much longer, billowed out behind her in the wind. A man passing by saw the skinny girl on the bicycle and thought to himself that she was more hair than girl.

When she did not arrive home on time, Tharshi was alarmed. Had the neighbors seen her? No. Tharshi walked up the hill into the village, to St. Anne's, to see if Uma's teachers knew where she was. None of them did, but when they saw the fear on Tharshi's face, they all came back down the hill with her to hunt for Uma.

Then Tharshi remembered that Uma had taken the bicycle.

THARSHI WALKED ALL OVER Kandy Road until she saw the place where the bushes had given way to something—or someone—careening out of control. And then she heard a scream she did not want to recognize. Tharshi found Uma by following the sound of that terrified voice. Picking her way through the brush and debris to her daughter.

Uma was crumpled under the bicycle, its weight seeming enormous above her small battered body. She was screaming, and this time the scream definitely had sound, sound so awful that Tharshi trembled and quivered and forgot her humiliation. She remembered the sound, had heard it before and did not know where, wanted more than anything for it to stop. But it was as though Uma was sleepwalking. They could not stir her. Eventually her voice ran out, and her hands bled where they clutched to the spokes on the bicycle wheel. They had to untangle her from the metal, cutting her shredded clothes away from her body and the wheels. Falling off the bicycle was not what had cut her so badly; it seemed to Tharshi that Uma had been clawing at herself. There were long scratch marks all over her too-small face, even near her too-big eyes, which were wide open and unseeing.

THEY TOOK UMA TO ANOTHER DOCTOR. And another. And another. They took her to a psychiatrist, who gave her drugs that did not work.

They took her to Neelan, who after one look at his sister became completely silent. He closed up his own practice and took her to a temple on the top of a mountain, where they saw an old and holy man. He tilted her face up, blessed her, and sprinkled her with sweet holy ash. This changed nothing, except perhaps to make the gods love her even more.

The gods took Uma for themselves.

The doctors took Uma from Tharshi and put her away.

YEARS LATER, WHEN THE little boy with the heart murmur grows up and becomes Dr. Murali and a father himself, I ask him about his family, especially his sisters, of whom I have heard almost nothing. We can recite all the names easily, but we want to know *what happened.* Tell me *what happened.* Did Uma become very famous? I know she was smart. Tell me what she did. Did she get married? Did she get a job? No one knows what happened to Uma. He answers the questions very slowly. He says: Uma got very sick. She went to the hospital, and she never left. In what is left of the small boy's memory, this is truth. But there is more.

What he does not say: *sometimes my sister Uma heard voices. Sometimes I worry that my children, their children will hear voices—although I should know better. I worry that you will hear her, that she will say—Hold my madness for me please.* What he does not say: that once, long ago, one of his relatives said to him that he thought Uma had been disappointed in Love, and that she had gone crazy because of it. That this was why she was UnMarried. Alone. Uma was not like Kunju, who had chosen to go bitter instead of crazy. Uma did not have a choice. The constellation of Uma's Brain had reconfigured itself; the auspicious stars had fallen out of alignment because Uma had been UnLoved.

His mother, Tharshi, is dead, but he knows what she would say if he repeated this story aloud. Tharshi, who loved Uma, would have said her youngest daughter was just Too Special to Get Married.

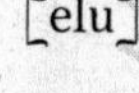

[elu]

VANI

EDGING EVER CLOSER

The words of the good are like a staff in a slippery place.

—TIRUKKURAL, *chapter 42, line 5*

IF THE STORY OF WHAT HAPPENED TO UMA WAS SHUT UP IN the cool and quiet cabinet of memory—as family secrets often are—then the story of what eventually happened to Vani's aunt Mayuri is entombed. It is buried so deep that to find it, you would have to walk halfway around the world, back to that teardrop country, and to the house where Vairavan's children used to live.

What happened after Dr. Bala walked down those porch steps for the last time? Mayuri's mother, Lakshmi, told her that Mr. Thiru, that meddling man, had been able to stop the Marriage because it was not meant to be. Mayuri shook off this explanation. She became a teacher. She lived at home for many years, and as her voice got louder and Lakshmi's got quieter, it slowly became Mayuri's house and not Lakshmi's. One day Lakshmi died and the village of Urelu, full as it had been of people who loved her and Vairavan, barely noticed, barely stopped to pay its respects.

What happened is that Mayuri became what is known in common parlance as a spinster, and a not very nice spinster at that. What happened is that Mayuri got very lonely, and very quiet, until one day, a new teacher sat down next to her at the noon meal, and she found to her own surprise that she had a friend.

THE FRIEND'S NAME WAS SHANTHI, and she was all by herself in the world. She was not Married. She had never been Married. She had no other friends because she had just moved to Urelu from Colombo. Mayuri looked across the table and saw part of herself in Shanthi. They were quickly so close that they seemed to form a family. Two women, UnMarried, without other attachments or obligations. They did everything together. The two spinsters vacationed together, shopped together, went out to movies together. Their names, when spoken of in the village's many households, became one. ShanthiMayuri. Coupled with Mayuri's older, more established family, Shanthi found herself with an automatic welcome at many doors that would not ordinarily have been open to her.

She was a strange woman. Had Mayuri been more observant, she might have seen that Shanthi had no other friends even after she had been there for years, and that although Mayuri's old friends did not ignore her, their voices grew formal when Shanthi entered the conversation. They did not like her; they did not trust her; they did not know her. They had no desire to know her. They did not understand why Mayuri loved her. If Mayuri had thought about it a little longer or a little harder, perhaps she would have seen that she too did not understand why she loved Shanthi.

But Mayuri loved her, and as always, Love is unreasonable. Shanthi was a snake charmer, and Mayuri loved Shanthi most because Shanthi had chosen her. Mayuri could not forget that once, a long time ago, someone had not.

THEY LIVED THEIR LIVES TOGETHER, and Mayuri, who once trusted no one, learned to trust again. She did not hesitate to give Shanthi anything. They were like sisters, after all, she thought. They opened a bank account together.

That was the first mistake.

It was commonly accepted that they were both a little crazy, maybe more than a little crazy. But Mayuri was the daughter of a good family, and so allowances were made. Every good teacher had her eccentricities. And Mayuri was a good teacher. She was also the oldest woman in Urelu to ride a bicycle, and it was a tandem she shared with Shanthi. She wore her hair loose, although that was considered odd in a woman of her age and standing, and her hair had not gone white, even by the time she was fifty-five. It still fell in thick, black, shiny locks around her face, which remained unwrinkled and unbeautiful. At school, the other teachers asked one another enviously if she dyed her hair and asked one another what she was using on her face to look like she was still thirty. She never spoke to men, except those who were related to her, unless it was a matter of urgent business.

And what my mother had thought about her—that she had allowed things to happen to her, rather than creating a life—became less true. Slowly, in choosing Shanthi, Mayuri chose the way her life formed around her. Shanthi held the trusting Mayuri so thoroughly in her thrall that those who had known Mayuri in her prickly youth thought the newcomer might as well have conjured up a new Mayuri entirely. They were familiar in a way that was more than sisterly. No one had ever seen a relationship quite like this before.

If they had seen the situation truly, they might have come to understand that Shanthi was not reviving Mayuri. She was—in a sense—killing her. Mayuri was too old for her brother to manage her affairs. Logan was a *dorai* now; he would not interfere. What she chose to do with the small fortune she had made by saving and investing was her own business.

ONE OF MAYURI'S STUDENTS was the first to notice that the crotchety English teacher was not quite herself. Every day she seemed less so. She was sick, he thought, and no one was going to take care of her. The boy had a Heart big enough to love even the meanest teacher. At the end of one school day, as he unloaded his books, he said to his mother that he did not like to see Miss Vairavan out of sorts. He thought she was ill. She had been coughing. She looked tired. At first his mother laughed at her son's concern, but then she thought about it. Her son was an observant child, a sharp child, and if he thought something was wrong, she was better safe than sorry.

She called her friend Sarojini, who was Mayuri's cousin.

FAMILY IS FAMILY, AND so Sarojini, although only a distant relation by Urelu standards, walked the path to Mayuri's one evening. She found her older cousin doubled over on the kitchen floor and her cup of tea smashed on the ground.

She was not just old.

But also sick.

Sarojini called Logan.

BUT BY NOW, LOGAN WAS IN CANADA. Eldest son–ship is difficult to exercise from abroad. He could not mistake the urgency in Sarojini's voice, but Mayuri insisted she was fine, and that her friend Shanthi could take care of her. Logan had little choice but to agree. Had he known the extent of the power his sister was relinquishing, he would have been appalled.

Shanthi pronounced Mayuri unfit to take care of any of her own affairs and said she would be caretaker. No one in Urelu wanted to contest that, especially when it was what Mayuri herself wanted. Power of attorney went to Shanthi. The bank account, once joint, went to Shanthi. The school no longer wanted Mayuri to teach but allotted her a generous pension, which went directly to Shanthi—as compensation, she noted, for a great service: nursing her sick friend would take a considerable amount of her time and she herself was an old woman. It would take so much of her time that it was determined that she could not continue teaching either. There would be enough of Mayuri's money to support them both.

THERE WERE LETTERS FIRST. Then phone calls. Whispers, in a barely recognizable accent. *She doesn't even feed me. She wants to sell the house—my house!* What? Who is this? Logan's daughter demanded into the receiver, and after that heard only a click.

NEARLY A YEAR LATER, Shanthi herself called Logan. *I'm an old woman. I'm tired. It's not my job to take care of your sister.* Fine, he said. I can arrange for family to see to her needs. It was all done; Logan flinched when he saw the drained bank account balance and heard from Sarojini how emaciated his sister looked and how well fed her friend seemed. Forget all that, he decided. *Let's get her out of there,* he whispered over the phone to Sarojini, who was so horrified at what was happening that she was remembering all over again that obligation sometimes brings love with it.

They got her out of there. She looked so happy to leave, Sarojini reported, and ate as though she had not eaten during her entire time with Shanthi. They made her sign an agreement not to see Shanthi again.

ONE MONTH LATER, LOGAN receives a panicked phone call: Mayuri has disappeared from her guardian's house—she had been left unattended for only one moment—she is gone—gone—gone. She is too strong now to have been taken against her will. She is still charmed by Shanthi. And Shanthi is still charmed by the promise of a free ride.

If you want to know what happened to Mayuri, there is only one person you can ask: Shanthi. And you have to find her first.

[ettu]

KUMARAN
NOT YET DEPARTED

Virtue will burn up the soul that is without love,
even as the sun burns up the creature that is without bone.

—TIRUKKURAL, *chapter 8, line 7*

MY MOTHER'S FATHER TOO WAS DEAD BEFORE SHE MARRIED. Aravindran's children called him Ayah, which in itself is unusual, meaning "sir" and not "father." Kumaran was thirteen when Ayah died. When he told me about it, his hair was gray and silver.

I can't really tell you about Ayah. I can only give you the perceptions of him I had when I was young. I wasn't at home when he died. I was boarded and studying at St. John's, in Jaffna proper. And very late one night, my uncle Logan came to the hostel unexpectedly. I came down to see him, and he said, Your father has expired.

I didn't cry; I think I didn't quite realize that Ayah was dead. I just got into the car and Logan drove and we went to Urelu. So that was the death. I think I cried during the ceremony. We performed the ritual acts for the dead. The younger children weren't allowed to go to the cremation ground itself. I think they thought it was just too much for us. So we stayed at home. I received a great many telegrams of condolence from my classmates. I think I really broke down when I got back to my school.

A few months later I stopped working at my school. I just stopped. And my class master called me up and said, You're not working anymore, and I said yes and he said, Do you realize that you're taking a valuable place that someone else would like to have, and I said, fine, I'll leave. And I left. That is, I went to see Logan, who was running the tea estates, and said I didn't want to study anymore. I wasn't interested in working on mathematical problems, which suddenly became very unreal to me after my father died. It seemed to have no importance.

So there you are. Kumaran stopped very suddenly and blinked.

I don't have very many memories of when he was alive. Just

a few, but they are very vivid. I would say he was an extremely emotional person, who could cry fairly easily, and this used to embarrass me. And as a result of this for a very long time after that I made myself unable to cry.

I saw him cry sometimes not from sadness, but out of pride in his family. I think he identified with them very strongly. Silly things could make him cry, like a cricket match between his extended family and the people in the area in which we used to live. If the family lost, he cried. If the family won, he cried. Ayah used to confide in me quite a lot because I was the only son, and I think after he died I had all of this knowledge that he held within himself. What my father had said to me about the honor and responsibility of being the eldest son and taking care of the family. I have never cried in the way my father did. It was as though my father had cried enough for all of us.

I also saw my father cry in the sort of mystic trance that quite a number of people in Jaffna used to get into. It was part of the way they related to what they called God. In the Nallur temple it was not unusual to go into a trance like this. I also have memories of following with him behind a guru, a saintly man, who was not living far from where we were. Often we did this. It would happen in the morning. It was like going for a walk. There were no words. The saintly man would lead. The others would follow a few steps behind. It was only later that I realized that these walks with my father and the guru corresponded to what we Hindus call *darshan*. The mere act of proximity, holiness rubbing off. The mystical aspect.

I remember only one negative thing about my father: Ayah telling off the cleaner, who was supposed to belong to the untouchable caste.

That more than bothered me. I had a sentiment of both injustice and rebellion against my father. In retrospect, I think I probably possess many of the same faults. I'm not going to go into details, but of course, I think I am totally free of any caste, color, or sexual prejudice. Not because I was like that always. But because of the kind of person I chose to be. It was a way in which I did not want to be like my father.

KUMARAN GREW AWAY FROM his family. He passed through many nations, no longer a citizen of Sri Lanka.

A few years after Ayah died, I told Logan, who now had authority over me as my mother's only brother, that I wanted to go to England. Why England? I certainly didn't want to do medicine, which was maybe the thing to do. Because I couldn't imagine spending my life dealing with sickness, misery, obliged to look at blood. So that was a flight. For part of my time there I worked as a trainee at a firm. We used to have quite a good time, the students at the office. We didn't do much work. We went to work at half past nine—tea at ten, back at eleven, out for lunch at twelve, back at one or two, out for tea again at half past three o'clock. We used to go and watch rugby matches, or sometimes cricket, on the weekends. Sometimes we went to the cinema. This was a time when I started drinking, not so much to get drunk, but because I thought I should learn to like the taste of beer. That it was a part of this world that I was trying to enter. And then I came back and got back into the engineering faculty at Jaffna. There was nothing positive about choosing engineering. It was just the only thing I could think of at that time that was still acceptable to the family, because it was a profession, but it enabled me to stay in Jaffna instead of going elsewhere for university. And I started to go into what I imagined was a real life.

This was also the time when the Sinhalese-Tamil problems came to the fore. Bandaranaike had come to power in 1956. But even at the Jaffna faculty, I had Sinhalese friends. Some of them were for parity, that Tamils should have equal access to education and to jobs. Some were against this, but they did not see this as a racial question at all, and I did have some friends who were against parity, but who were really my friends.

But I had seen what could happen. When I was younger, I was sent to Colombo to live with one of my father's cousins, who was an engineer. This was very shortly after my father had died, and the idea was that his cousin would guide me back to something productive. That if I was unwilling to go to school, I would learn to work. I lived at his house in Wellawatte, which is a Tamil section in Colombo, and I went to the office with him every morning.

And that summer, there were anti-Tamil riots. One morning the trouble was quite bad, and he told me I shouldn't go to work. But after he left, I followed him to work, because I was too restless to stay at home.

Sometime after I arrived at the office, a mob formed and surrounded the building where we were working.

KUMARAN WAS A JAFFNA TAMIL by birth. He had a skinny face and the same toothy, quick, white smile that his father had had, but his smile looked much whiter because he was very dark, as though the steady equatorial sun had imprinted itself permanently on his skin. He had a stocky build and that solid jaw. In Sri Lanka, his entire physical character meant that he was something unusual: he fell into the space between the ethnic assumptions people were willing to make. He was not always recognized as a Jaffna Tamil. It is not that Kumaran wasn't anyone. But all his life he had a shape shifter's gift for being mistaken for anyone. The ease of acquiring language and gesture. Becoming whoever was most convenient. And this was part of what later made him valuable to the Tigers.

There were three men in charge of the office where he was working that summer in Colombo. One was Charles Gunasekera, and he was a Sinhalese. The other two were Tamil, and one was Kumaran's cousin. Kumaran had watched Charles help them to hide but had done nothing to hide himself, although the whole office could hear the mob coming. They were holding torches, and Kumaran thought about the roofs of faraway Jaffna, some of which were made of leaves and could be easily burned.

When the mob came, Charles Gunasekera went out onto the steps and calmly said that the two Tamil men, the friends whom he had hidden, were not there. Kumaran watched him. He did not know Charles Gunasekera, but after a moment, he went out onto the steps and joined him.

Probably the fact that I'm not obviously a Tamil by my physical origin saved me from a beating, Kumaran said slowly. It was foolish. I was a young boy. When we went home, my cousin was furious. He said, *I told you not to go.* But I had been protected by this cloak of ethnic anonymity.

Kumaran paused, and I thought: But that was so arbitrary. We look alike.

Later, Kumaran said, after the riots got worse, the government put the Tamil refugees on a ship that took them around the country to Point Pedro, back north.

One of the things that disgusted me on this ship was that after having spent a number of days as refugees because they were seen to be Tamils, the Tamils who were on this ship were still following their caste prejudices. So I thought to myself, maybe we deserve what we get.

I have to tell you that when he told me about his youth, what he said about having no prejudices, I did not believe him. If that was true, why did he try to stop my father?

BUT KUMARAN DID NOT really think this was true, that Tamils deserved what had happened to them. He remembered his time in England and what it had been like there.

When I got to the U.K. I had a shock. Very soon I realized that I had become a colored person. Worse than being a Tamil in Sri Lanka, in some ways, because they could pick me out as different on the street. And at first I was unable to find a firm willing to accept me as an apprentice while I was studying.

At the end of three months, with my money running out, I finally found a place. Initially, I spent my time drinking a lot of beer and chasing a lot of girls and not doing any work at all. I liked this experience a lot.

At this job, Kumaran met Muttiah, who later married into the family of the current president of Sri Lanka. And so Kumaran had entrée to what was a salon of sorts. He was particularly affected by Muttiah himself, as well as another man to whom he was introduced, an elderly gentleman who was a former member of the Communist Party and an ex-intelligence agent. This man was an anarchist, but did not believe in violence, and Kumaran, riot residue still in his brain, was beginning to disagree. Kumaran was surrounded by this group of people, lived with them, breathed with them. He was still a boy from Urelu, who still remembered everything that had happened to him there, whereas his older friend, Muttiah, had entirely rejected Sri Lanka and the East. This was something that Kumaran had no desire or ability to do. The elderly gentleman edited a monthly magazine. Kumaran began to write for it, and to think very hard about politics. Later he would come to articulate his deep revulsion toward anything race- or caste-based.

After a year, almost by accident and without a great deal of studying, he managed to pass his courses. It was time to go back.

BECAUSE HE STILL DID not have very much money, he decided to make the trip overland. It turned out to be a pilgrimage of sorts. It was just before this trip that Kumaran fell in Love. Because he was Kumaran he fell in Love Twice. The first time began in a bookshop. A few days earlier, he had heard from a friend who was very upset. The friend had met a beautiful girl in a bookshop. But she would not give him her telephone number, and now he could not find her, although he had gone back to the bookstore for many days, hoping to see her again. Not long after talking to this friend, Kumaran went into this bookshop himself to buy a copy of a political journal. He saw a girl matching his friend's description standing in the magazine aisle. She was fair-haired and she wore boots that made her seem taller than she was. She had a sculptured face, a face he might have seen wandering in a museum. Her mouth was shiny, red, and slick. She wore rectangular-framed black glasses on the bridge of her nose.

Kumaran went up to her and introduced himself by telling her who she was. (You're Justine. I know. But who are you? I don't know you.) In the course of one conversation with her Kumaran persuaded her to go to India with him. Later his persuasive abilities would be of great use to the Tigers. He was not yet in Love with her, although he liked her shiny fair hair, her serious black glasses, and her red mouth, which was the opposite of serious. She had been reading a magazine to which he subscribed. He thought she was someone with whom he could be friends.

A few months later she asked him to go to Paris with her on the way to India. She was French and wanted to go home. His friend, the man who had seen her in the first place, did not come with them.

At Heathrow, a brusque customs officer stopped her.

Where are you going?

To Paris.

With whom, madam?

My boyfriend.

What is his name? Where does he live? This gentleman?

But the agent already knew Kumaran's name. Kumaran was standing right there. Justine took a deep breath.

Don't you have any English friends? Why don't you travel with them? the customs agent was yelling. It's people like you, madam, who are causing a problem in this country.

Love turns Political sometimes. From the airport, Kumaran called up a left-wing newspaper to tell them about the incident. The story made a small scandal. Someone in London saw it, clipped it, and anonymously sent it to his family in Sri Lanka. Vani opened the envelope and read it and pressed her lips together. In Paris, Kumaran found a letter responding to the article, a letter saying *Go back where you came from.*

Political Love. Or rather, Love under the strain of politics. Kumaran was fed up with London, with Paris, with Europe. He could not stop himself from wanting home.

KUMARAN THOUGHT HE MIGHT be falling in Love with Justine himself. From Paris they went to Geneva, and then to Venice. They took a boat to Istanbul and talked about politics. He sensed in her a willingness to be radical. She sang to herself in French on the deck of the ship, and when she went below deck with him, her hair kept the fragrance of the salt wind. He thought she might like to go home with him. She was French, and they were in Love. She decided to go to Sri Lanka with him. He had felt guilty about none of this so far, but now, when he thought of his childhood sweetheart, Meenakshi, waiting for him, he felt conscience stab him. He thought about writing her a letter and didn't.

They took a boat from Istanbul to Erzurum. Then they rode a bus to the Iranian border. From there they hitchhiked on lorries to Tehran. In Tehran they met some Albanian men who were driving to Pakistan. They agreed to share expenses and hitched a ride. Then they took a train to the border of India, where the customs agent looked up and down scornfully at Kumaran.

Who are you going to see?

My mother.

And this answer prompted the customs agent to ask why Kumaran was taking a white girl home to see his mother. Kumaran did not say anything in response, but inside he was furious and mortified: the customs agent was still speaking in English; Justine understood everything. He hoped she was not too offended, because he really did want to marry her.

FROM THERE THEY WENT to Delhi, where they were delayed for nearly a week as Kumaran tangled with the Indian secret police, who suspected that he was a Pakistani spy. In retrospect, this seems less ridiculous than it did then. When the matter was finally cleared up, by way of apology the police booked them berths to Madras. From Madras to Rameshwaram, and from there to Thanushkodi. Back then to get to Thanushkodi you took the ferry, and as you crossed from India to Sri Lanka you could see the very big rocks that rise out of the sea. In mythology it is supposed to be the rest of the bridge built by the god Hanuman to rescue the damsel Sita.

But Justine stopped at Rameshwaram.

How long has it been since you have been home? she asked him.

About a year. More or less, he said.

I think you should go alone, she said. I'll wait here for you. You can send for me after a while.

He shrugged. He needed to get home.

When he arrived alone in Jaffna, he saw that his mother and Vani were glad to see him, and he was happier than he had realized he would be to see them. After Jaffna he went to Colombo to visit Kalyani. His older sister was angry to see him. But this was not because of Justine. She alone knew about Justine, but her anger ran deeper.

You have no right to come here after going away for so long, Kalyani said.

BUT HE HAD ACTUALLY become more Sri Lankan by going away. Once, in London, Kumaran had met a woman who was not yet an MP in Sri Lanka, who was a student at a British university. They were at a party at the Sri Lankan ambassador's house, and Kumaran, who would never learn to Shut Up, managed to silence the crowd by telling her that her father, then a racist Sri Lankan Cabinet minister, deserved whatever trouble he got. She was taken aback by the young man with the shock of dark hair who was so vehemently damning her. Kumaran was once a fighter, but even when he became physically violent, he still fought best with words. His time in England made him a scrapper, a plotter: a negotiator. And he did not die of a war wound, or in the political line of duty.

AFTER VISITING KALYANI IN COLOMBO, Kumaran wrote to Justine and told her not to come to Sri Lanka. He returned to Jaffna and its university. Then, in 1976, he was gone. No one ever heard from or of Justine again, although it seemed for a time that Meenakshi's mournful face was everywhere. She was a classmate of Vani's, but Vani never spoke to her, although after she was killed, Kumaran's whole family went to her funeral.

NEARLY TWENTY YEARS LATER, a doctor who was sympathetic to the cause told Kumaran that he had terminal cancer. You cannot escape your blood. And after being told this news, Kumaran was finally ready to leave the Tigers, to follow the family he had not seen in so long. To leave the country. Victor provided him with false identification papers: a humane gesture from a man who should have forgotten how to be humane by this time. And Kumaran went to Canada, where he lived in hiding, but not alone. He brought his daughter with him.

He wrote letters to his family, not caring, finally, whether they were traced, whether he was found, knowing only that he wanted to see them again. He did; they came from all over the Western world to see him. *Kumaran machan. Kumaran Anna.* Our Kumaran, our darling, our dear. *Is it really you?* He was clean-shaven again for the first time in years and did not look like the wartime pictures of himself, those photographs in which he had always been in the periphery. They did not speak of the war; he did not want to talk about it. *Tell me about yourselves, your husbands, your children.* He was already beginning to lose weight and hair, his bones emerging from his body like an omen. They were with him, around him, when he died: his sisters.

Shortly after his death, the Tigers turned down an offer that was just short of what they wanted: not secession, but a northern government with greater autonomy. His sisters barely paid attention, barely noticed, because Kumaran was dead. As Vairavan's murder had been an introduction to violence, this was a farewell: this, the cancer stripping Kumaran's bones, his blood, his vision going in the final days. They had no eyes for the news, only him, their amazing vanishing brother.

My father, Murali, deals every day in people who will die. This is his business. My father's patients die. They die, and he has not lost the ability to be moved by this, as some doctors do.

His patients die. They die young, not from bombs or guns or wars, but by themselves, by their bodies' betrayals. As Kumaran did, in the end. If one of his patients dies, my father will go to the funeral and transform himself from a doctor to a mourner. This is not a person (formerly). He passed that test long ago. Look at the body and make it no one. *No.* Not anymore. This is a body he has tended to as though his own, a body he has known, not in a sexual way, but in a paternally intimate way. More than a body. He is older now, and he has chosen to make the bodies he treats back into people, knowing already the burden this carries.

Choosing to die in a certain way is a mark of honor in some cultures. This is not difficult to understand. Martyrdom is something crusaders secretly dream of: to fall, with honor, with a name. Anonymous martyrdom, on the other hand, is something very different. Kumaran died without a name, without choosing the manner in which he would die. Just a man, no longer a soldier. Whether he is a martyr or not: I cannot say.

THE INTERSECTION OF WAR and love is a strange place. No one outside the Tigers ever knew who Janani's mother was, because Kumaran did not tell anyone. He had a year with us before he died, and he said barely a word. I suppose he had had in those twenty years a lot of practice in keeping secrets. Perhaps he wanted to keep her to himself. Perhaps he saw her in his daughter, and that was enough.

Janani: from the beginning, she was uncannily like two people: her father, and me. She was four years younger than me, but except for being paler and considerably thinner, she was almost identical. She was fluent in Tamil, less so in English. She spoke a little Sinhalese. She never actually asked for her mother, but I felt noble, sharing mine. My parents helped her plan her wedding, and her father's funeral.

Even now, in the middle of this, in the middle of all this: parents conducting the concert of Arranged Marriage. Parents want nothing more than to prevent their children from colliding with inevitability: that in a different world, there is a different kind of marriage, in which you do not and cannot marry a family. Parents Tamil and Sinhalese watch helplessly as their children cut themselves free of the need to please their ancestors. They walked out of their country to give us opportunity, but this was not the opportunity they intended us to take: American Marriage. We live by our own wits, our own hearts, and our own histories; there is no other way to survive here, and so we have learned to love people who do not worship our gods, eat our food, or share our blood. Our children are children of two races, sometimes of two religions, often of three countries.

In his last years of life, Kumaran privately renounced his ties to the Tigers, but he was still one of them. He told my parents he was sorry for what he had done to them; sorry for the letter he had written my father, threatening his life; sorry for everything.

And still, in this globe-scattered Sri Lankan family, we speak of only two kinds of marriage. The first is the Arranged Marriage. The second is the Love Marriage. In reality, there is a whole spectrum in between, but most of us spend years running away from the first toward the second.

Most of us. Not Janani. In Toronto, she passed through crowds without acknowledging those watching her—afraid of nothing, moved by nothing. She was among us, but still not one of us.

I MUST GO OUTSIDE myself to see that before Kumaran and Janani returned, we lived a quiet life. In America, Marriage has not been a way out and fear has not been a way of living. Houses don't burn—at least not for the same reasons. But Love, or rather Sex, is everywhere. Murali's Heart has stopped murmuring, but he has never quite reconciled it with this impropriety. So when Sex in its many forms blares out at him, he covers his eyes, and those of his daughter, who is already failing to understand an older, more conservative world.

He did not come to this country so that his child could fall in Love so Improperly. His daughter, Vani's daughter, is beloved. She has Uma's brains, Mayuri's prickliness, and underneath it all, Harini's steel. She has his Heart. But they know that she is perhaps most like Uma. More like Uma than he would prefer, although this is something he only admits in the dark. No one has said Uma's name aloud for years. Just as Kumaran was once only a phantom.

AND NOW, MURALI REMEMBERS what Uma and Kumaran were like, their younger selves, as he watches me travel the distance between myself and my uncle. And yet this descent is different from Uma's long absence and Kumaran's long silence. But I too enter my room and close the door, shut everyone else out. I am more at home with a pen than a person. Murali sees this and is not sure what to do. Murali remembers his brother Neelan taking Uma to the temple, remembers Uma's blank eyes as the priest sprinkled holy ash on her forehead. Uma was not there, not there to the point that when the temple lamp was passed she dipped her fingers into the fire instead of hovering at its edge. She did not notice the pain. Murali knows now that you cannot escape your demons. He sees me, Yalini, as perhaps most like Uma: she has those otherworld eyes.

JANANI: SHE WEARS ANOTHER Wedding-Red sari, like a red ghost out of history. She tries it on, and my mother and my aunt drape and redrape her. Tomorrow they will go to the wedding hall, begin to lay out the lamps and the flowers in preparation for the ceremony.

The chatter around the bride is loud. They plait her hair, fasten her anklets, and thread flower after flower onto garlands. As Murali did long ago, the groom has built the altar himself. The sound of a wedding, the sound of a going. I clasp a necklace around Janani's neck, pat down her sari and straighten it.

[ompathu]

JANANI AND YALINI
FINALLY THEIR DAUGHTERS

To discern the truth in everything,
by whomsoever spoken, this is wisdom.

—TIRUKKURAL, *chapter 43, line 3*

CHILDREN ARE BORN TO BE MARRIED. TO HAVE THEIR OWN children.

At my birth, to my father, Murali, I looked like his mother, Tharshi, with her high brow. My dark head gleamed under the glaring hospital lights. Murali felt his Heart traveling out of his possession and, with a sigh, let it go. A daughter born in this country, the wrong country, has so much more of a chance. He loved looking down at this bright bundle in his arms. I had only the faintest eyebrows—disappearing eyebrows, like my mother's—and a lower lip with a full pout, like my grandmother's. I could have been any and all of them, and I was: Uma, Harini, Mayuri, Tharshi. I could have been Vani. I could and would be anything. He loved the world of possibility in my newborn face, which was unknown and yet already familiar.

According to custom, when they brought me home, they shaved my head. Murali held me still, and Vani traced the razor gently over the curve of my baby skull. It is said that hair will grow back stronger after this. I was very quiet. In contrast to Janani, who my uncle told me was a plump, crying baby, I rarely cried. The cutting of my hair was only the first of many transformations. Perhaps they knew it then, but I would not become beautiful. I began by looking like Vani but ended by looking like Murali. I am not pretty. I have his oval face, but his features on me look undistinguished. I do not have Vani's high cheekbones or finely structured features. I was born with dark eyes that became lighter every day.

My father wanted to take me home to Sri Lanka; he wished that his mother could see me. Day after day, the experience of watching me did not lose any of its wonder. From my earliest months I showed myself to be among the quickest of children. I laughed ahead of schedule, talked ahead of schedule. My mother, a teacher, took great pains in reading to me every night. And she saw her aunts in my many sides. She had not seen them for so long, and to see them now in this small person, this small person who was hers, was very strange. It had been a very long time since she had lived in Jaffna, she realized.

Because they could not take me to the fine, white sand beaches at home, they took me to the American beaches. It was all so familiar, but also so wrong in many ways. It was filled with the wrong people. The sand was not the right color—not the almost-pure-whiteness of a Ceylonese beach, but rather tea-colored, as if it were the dregs of my mother's cup. Here people sought out the sun, trying to get darker. Their sisters had guarded their skin from the sun and massaged Fair & Lovely into their faces. I scampered bareheaded out of the shade of the umbrella that my father had planted in the sand like a flag. My mother started to say something and then bit her lower lip. This is not a beach, Murali thought. He wanted to take us home. He wanted to see his own mother. He wanted Tharshi to meet Vani.

IN 1985, THE ONLY TIME I have ever been to Sri Lanka, flying home took more than a day. I was only two and my father wondered if I would remember this trip when I grew up. He thought I would not, and he was right. He wanted to take me anyway. Later he was glad he did. It was four years after the burning of the Jaffna Library, and two years after Black July. In a few more years, the war would kick off again in earnest, and Ariyalai and Urelu would empty of young people. My parents returned to the island understanding that this was good-bye. But after all, how does one say good-bye to a place? My father asked himself this later. For the moment, conversations were not burdened with farewells. Murali moved within the sphere of his family, delighted with the sense of *belonging again.* He had forgotten what it was like to speak without repeating himself. He had forgotten the gentle sound of British vowels in Tamil voices. He had forgotten his mother's quiet strength and height—forgotten that even in her old age, she was nearly as tall as him and as tall as his father had been.

He watched with pleasure his mother and his daughter's fascination with each other. Tharshi picked me up, held me close to her, and inhaled my sweet powder fragrance, mingled with her own faint aroma of jasmine and sandalwood. She reached out a dry finger and I curled a moist fist around it. It was then that my father could see the beginning of his father's steady gaze on my face, for I did grow to look like my father, and therefore his father too. I reached out for the diamond glittering in Tharshi's nose, and she gasped with unexpected pain and surprise. I chirped up at my grandmother: *What's this? what's this?* My mother did not have a *mūkkutti,* and I did not remember ever seeing one. My father laughed at the expression on Tharshi's face and disengaged my hand from my grandmother's nose. That was not very nice!

he scolded gently. Tharshi rubbed a hand over her nose where I had tugged it and chuckled: *Kulapadi!* Naughty girl.

On the third day that we were there, my mother's sister, Kalyani, brought my cousins to visit us, and all of us went to the beach. We piled into an old car borrowed from a neighbor and drove down the road, rattling away. When my father pulled over, my mother was the first to open the door and step into the sand. She inhaled with pleasure and excitement, and this did not escape her watchful husband. *So soft. So warm*, said his Heart, which had been well for a long time. *What are you doing here?* It was a Heart glad to be warm again. I followed my cousins into a reedy part of the sea, and my father watched us dip our hands into the water. Later I saw the picture he took of us playing there. In the picture we are all very happy and dirty, our hair beginning to clump with salt, and sand gathering on our skin and under our fingernails. We are all smiling missing-tooth smiles. My face is still round and fair, my hair short. I am two years old, innocently naked to the waist, gleeful, my hands full of shells. It is one of the few candid family pictures; most of them are posed with smiles frozen on for a special occasion.

Very shortly after my father took the photograph I was no longer smiling. A jellyfish in the shallow waves bit my ankle. An angry red mark, not quite the shade of a Wedding-Red sari, swelled up on my foot. My father took us home. I cried all the way there.

THERE WAS A DAY in that trip to my parents' birthplace when my father was missing. My mother did not tell us where he went, and no one mentioned it. I was too young and fascinated with this new place to see his absence. I spent that day playing in the garden as usual. My mother and grandmother sewed on the porch, the sound of insects a quiet hum behind our high-pitched chatter. I looked at some of the old family albums with my mother. The pictures were all very small and square, sepia-toned. My mother told me later that I mistook a picture of Jegan for my father. They had looked very much alike. There were no pictures of Uma in the album, but I was too young then to know the difference. I did not know anything or anyone was missing. And as we were there in the house at Ariyalai with my grandmother, my father was on a train, traveling toward his sister, who had not been entirely forgotten.

Uma was in a home only a few hours away. Over the years, Tharshi had gone to visit her daughter sometimes, but the Uma of those days was not the brilliant Uma of many years ago. She was dull-eyed and slower, the powerful drugs the doctors had given her coursing through her veins. Sometimes when Tharshi visited her, she brought food. Uma sat there and ate, and Tharshi talked to her and told her all the news of her family. But after a while, Tharshi realized that Uma was not listening to her. Often, her daughter's head was cocked to one side, as though she was listening to something else, something that only she could hear.

When we went to my father's home in 1985, he had not seen Uma since his childhood. He did not even know where she was. When he asked his mother about it, he saw in her face that she had become resigned to what had happened to her youngest and most cherished daughter. It no longer had the power to shock her, as it once had.

She told my father how to find Uma.

Later, my father was very glad that in his last trip home he had insisted on seeing his sister. She was older than he, but as he saw her sitting in her room that had been her home for so many years now, he knew that he had outgrown her. He saw that his sister was surrounded by objects connected to the world of civilization and order: broken pen nibs, half-filled notebooks, shelves of books Tharshi had sent to her over the years, and piles of letters tied with brown twine. The room was immaculate, with the exception of the desk at which she sat. Before her, stacks of paper rose in untidy towers. Fountain pens lay astray. Her cheeks, more hollow now than they had been when she was a girl, were marked with inky fingerprints. He saw that the desk was Uma's center, and it was a place of orderly things arranged in a disorderly way. He saw the slender thread of her connection to the world outside her barred window fraying.

He was older than Uma now, he realized. He wanted to cry but could not. He remembered a sister who had been quiet, her eyes always looking elsewhere. But he also remembered a sister who had been able to communicate that she knew herself and where she was, a sister who had once been very much in this world. He saw now that she was passing out of it. He saw that while her eyes had not lost their otherworld-ness, they were not as quick as they had once been. She wore glasses now. Her hair was still very long, but now it was silver.

When my father went to see Uma, she did not recognize him. He had told himself that he did not expect her to know him, but when she looked at him with no sign of recognition, his Heart sighed. *It's me,* the Heart said. *Murali. Thambi.* Little brother. We come from the people who share our blood. But she did not remember him.

He had brought her a photograph of his family. Himself and

Vani, me in my mother's lap. It was a studio photograph, posed, all of us meticulously combed and polished. He had labeled it on the back, laboring to make his doctor's hand legible. *Murali Thambi, Vani Thangachi, Yalini. 1985.* Uma did not speak to him, but he walked over to the desk and laid the photograph down on it.

YEARS LATER, WHEN THARSHI was sick, my father's brother Neelan went to see her. Tharshi already knew that she would not see my father or his family again. Murali, her youngest, had come—without knowing it—to say good-bye. And so it was Neelan who talked to his mother until her voice drifted off.

He thought she had fallen asleep. No—she reached out a hand and laid it on his arm. Wait a moment, *rasa.* She moved her hands to her ears and began to unscrew the earrings from her lobes. Neelan knew these as the diamonds that had caught his father's eye so long ago. She pressed them into his hand. Give these to Yalini for me.

I did not receive the gift until many years later, when Neelan and his family came for the first time to visit us in America. I watched my uncle take a small, silk drawstring bag from the pile of gifts he had brought us. He gave it to me and gestured for me to open it. The earrings tumbled into my hands, the pure, clear Ceylonese diamonds sparkling far more brilliantly than the American stones my parents had already given me. The daughters of Jaffna Tamils have always been given jewels, although they are no longer used as part of the ritual of dowries. Gifts like this usually come from within the family, but somehow I knew these were not from my uncle. Your grandmother wanted you to have them, he said by way of explanation. The earrings were set in very old gold, the posts thick in the traditional style. They did not fit into my narrowly pierced ears. My mother took them from me and turned them over in her palm. We'll have them remade for you, she said. They had already been remade once, although I did not yet know the story of how these diamonds had been plucked from Kunju's misshapen ears.

My aunt Kalyani took the diamonds with her on a trip to India, and when she returned after a few months, she brought the remade earrings: very old diamonds in a new setting. These earrings were smaller than Tharshi's had been. Some of the diamonds had been removed, combined with rubies, and made into a heavy pendant. I knew without asking that although my grandmother, whom I do not remember, wore these diamonds almost every day of her life, here in America they are the kind of gems I should wear only to a wedding. To do otherwise would be tempting God to take away such a gift. Across oceans, a grandmother long gone reached out to hand an heirloom to her granddaughter.

AND I WILL HAVE PLACES to wear these diamonds: wedding after wedding after wedding.

All families start with a marriage, and all marriages start with a family. Perhaps this is why before my family goes to weddings my mother insists on taking family photographs. We all look so lovely, she says. No—this is not what she means. For the rest of her life my mother will be racing to replace the irreplaceable: the photographs of her family that burned with her sister's house in 1983 in Sri Lanka. Ask my mother what she would take with her if the house was on fire, and she will not take a minute to consider the question: she would take the photographs. Of course.

Many of the photographs of her younger days, before she came to America, are missing; she did not bring very many of them to America when she came. There are perhaps ten pictures of my mother and her brother and sister. Once there were three of them. Now there are two. My uncle Kumaran, no longer a Tamil Tiger, died of cancer; it was one of the times I saw my mother cry. I look like her when I cry: our faces crumple as if they are burning paper.

Now his daughter, Janani, is getting Married. For me this means another transformation. For years my mother has stitched sari blouses, but none of them have ever been for me. Now I am too old to disregard the rules of decorum: although I would prefer not to be pushed into adulthood, she wraps a bolt of silk around me and drapes my hips, my shoulders, in bright cloth. I watch it happen in a mirror. My mother's mouth is full of pins. My aunt Kalyani stands with her hands on her hips in a corner, studying the fit. A little loose here, she suggests. I fight the urge to move, to arrange my body in some other, less revealing configuration.

A GIRL WHO LOOKS like her father instead of her mother is a girl who is unsure of who she should be. I had to learn to write in the first person. It is not something that comes to me naturally. I am a scientist, with a researcher's love of detail, third person, and distance. But you cannot write about your family without writing about yourself. You must be willing to say everything, always. In a moment of comfort I might allow someone like Uma to disappear and be forgotten. I might allow Tharshi's twin, Kunju, who was disfigured by a fire, to disappear and be forgotten. I want someone to read this later, to see that I love my family, even my uncle.

I only vaguely remember learning to read. My mother, Vani, taught me, and perhaps the reason I do not remember it clearly is because it was not like learning at all. It was knowing—just knowing. It happened all at once, like the sudden downpour of rain in the summer. I never had to guess what something meant. A word in a sentence was like a child in a family—my family: composed and defined by the other words, the way I am composed and defined by the other people in my family. My words always knew one another and were defined in relation to one another, and once I knew what they meant, each word took on a color and a memory of its own. I learned words and hoarded them away. I loved their shapes and hues and the way they felt full and round, and how ink looked sharp and clean on a white page. Words had answers.

By the time I was three years old I could read. I liked especially to have my mother read aloud to me before I went to bed. Sometimes I would read to her. Sitting on the bed beside her, I listened to her voice or my voice thread its way through a story. After a while, when I knew the story by heart, I would sit and think not about the narrative or the characters, but about the pure pleasure of that quiet sound cutting through the air. It was like the *darshan* my uncle had spoken of. The holiness transferred to anyone near it. It was like taking a walk right into a sound. It was a beautiful sound, because when we read, our voices were clear and measured each word, making it distinct in its own depth. I could distance myself from my own voice so that it turned into both motion and stillness, and I rocked in the transparent wall of sound and story, loving it. There was beauty especially in the ritual: selecting a book as she braided her hair, crossing my ankles on my bed and waiting for her, opening the first page together. I felt myself expand within this, welling up with stories remembered and stories I did not know I anticipated. I held them like sweet, glad secrets: Harini's beauty. Tharshi's twin. Uma's madness. Neelan's wife. Logan's tea. My father's love.

My mother could keep me occupied for a weekend by letting me borrow thirty books from the library. I loved the libraries—we had two in town, and each had its own cast of librarians and special, hidden places where books waited for me. The librarians loved me—almost could not believe their good fortune in finding a child who wanted to read everything. I remember what they looked like then, but I no longer know their names. You've grown again, they said when they saw me, although I had never been away more than a week. Sometimes I sat for hours, poring over the medical dictionary.

The old rugs and musty paper odor of libraries seemed very familiar to me, and I loved the sense of being an oasis moving within that great age. My mother would only allow me to borrow as many books as I could carry. How ridiculous I must have looked: a tiny, thin girl with enormous braids and glasses, bent under the beautiful weight of those books. We would come home, me lugging the torn blue-and-white canvas bag, straining at its seams with a few dozen books sticking out at odd angles.

The moment we were inside, I would run downstairs where, in one corner, there was a sliding glass door to the garden. If I drew the curtain back, and the day was sunny, I could position myself in the path of a certain patch of light, whose shape and angle and warmth pleased me. I placed my book into the pooling light and disappeared into the pages so deeply that I did not hear if my mother called me for dinner—or a friend called me to play a game—or my father came home from work.

I read quickly. I read everything—anything I could get my hands on. When I misbehaved, my mother punished me by forbidding me to read. I learned the many ways and places in which you could hide a book. Under a mattress is easy and even expected. If you cross your hands across your chest, concealing a book against the stomach is also possible. I liked to leave a book behind the dogwood tree in the garden. Sometimes, while cleaning, my mother found poetry or novels behind the mirror on my bureau. Or inside a kitchen cabinet. Although my mother did not let me read some things because she thought them too worldly, she did not catch everything. So I was a child with an old soul. I think sometimes I knew too much. Every day, when I came home from school, I would sit in the kitchen and read the newspaper straight through. Every story.

Whether any of those stories were as true as this one is another matter entirely. And so I come, finally, to the first person, and to the end and the beginning of the story. Reverse a family tree, and branches of blood are whittled down to one person. I am composed of all the women and men who came before me. I am the result of many Marriages.

TAMIL HAS TWO HUNDRED and forty-seven letters. When I was five years old, I could recite about half of them. I could speak Tamil and understand it. But as I got older, I forgot the words. I do not remember how this happened. Sometimes when I dream, I dream in Tamil. But when I wake up I never remember the words. It is like remembering a fever, or a blessing.

Even my father has begun to think in English. When I was younger there was a sense of shame in being too connected to a country that was not officially my own. I wanted to be American. I mastered English and went out of my way to tell people I had been born in America. When my parents went to the ethnic marketplace to buy the special spices my mother used in cooking, I stayed in the car and waited for them. When my parents got back in the car, they would smell of curry leaves, saffron, and cardamom. These odors were strange and strong. At home, my mother burned candles so that the house would not hold the fragrance. In Toronto, I learned to seek out the signs of Tamilness: the food, the people, the temples, the customs. Generations before me, Kunju sang for her education. My parents had had to force me to sing the devotionals she had known by heart. The only song I learned without protest was the Sri Lankan national anthem. I sang it once at the temple.

All the women cried except my mother.

I WAS BORN into a community of Sri Lankan doctors, their spouses, and their children. None of us yet knew how my family would drift away from this. In the winter, the cold made my mother's feet hurt. It was part of the reason we eventually left for a warmer climate. Her warm island soul hated the icy temperatures. In the new place, we were the only Sri Lankans.

In the years since we moved away from that first house I have had a recurring dream: I wake up and move through all the rooms of the house. My navigation is rough, my internal compass askew. I bump into walls and tables, bruising myself. I am no more than eight years old, and the architecture of the house is shadowy and fluid. The walls are not where I remember them. I cannot keep track of where I am. I keep hearing the sounds of people all around me—my mother in the kitchen, cooking breakfast. I can hear my father on the phone with someone at the hospital. But they are only sounds. I follow each one, but the sizzle of the stove vanishes as I enter an empty kitchen. The phone is off the hook. My father is not there. His footprints are pressed firmly into the carpet. He is gone.

I had this dream for the first time just before we moved. I woke up cold and sweating, feeling sick to my stomach. I pushed the sheets away and put one tentative foot on the smooth hardwood floor. I went from room to room methodically, checking for anyone—anyone. I thought no one was home; the house was silent. Each room upstairs was empty, the impressions of bodies in beds the only hint of a presence. By the time I went down the stairs, I was almost in tears—but there, finally, was my mother. She was confused and worried by my panic. I was glad to see her and to know that the walls would not start to shift around me.

I have been back to see that house only once since we left. My parents had to point the house out to me. The door used to be red. The new owners have repainted it black.

EVEN INSIDE MY OWN FAMILY, I am a scientist. The doctor's first order of business: do a history.

When I ask about family, it is my father who pours out his story. I am surprised—by my father, who rarely surprises me. It is my mother's family that has surrounded me and gathered me into its fold. But my father's distance from his family—which is scattered from here, to Sri Lanka, Australia, England, Germany, France, and Canada—gives him perspective. From his distance, he can dislike, he can like, he can judge, he can love, and he can praise with praise that means something because it is measured against those parts of his history that he does not remember with affection.

Sprawled across a bed in Paris, where we are visiting relatives, my father and I lie shoulder to shoulder, looking at the black book in which I have recorded what I know about the names and histories of our family. I listen to him reel off names, stumbling as he touches the outer fringes of his bloodlines. He does not remember all of their names. This is something that my mother finds astonishing, even shameful. But my father, I have discovered, does not collect names. He collects personalities, like pearls, with all the shading and beautiful, real imperfections of those jewels. It is like the way my parents' families kiss their children differently. My mother's family kisses in, pressing with their noses as though they can inhale you. My father's family kisses out, with their lips puckered and loud, hiding nothing. But my father hesitates, watching me record his words. And my mother outright stops when she sees my pen move across paper, noting what she says about an old rift between two branches of the family.

Why are you writing that down?

The three of them—my aunt, my cousin, my mother—look at me, alarmed. We are all clustered around the kitchen table, bathed in sunlight made brighter by snowfall. We are drinking tea. Always tea.

Why are you writing that down?

For history. To know, I say.

There's no need to keep an old grudge, my mother says.

I'm not keeping the grudge, I protest. I'm just recording it.

They do not understand this: *history.* Cure the future by knowing the past. Even my cousin, who is only a few years older than I, cedes to their side. Later, in my room, upstairs, I write down what my mother said anyway. If it is not recorded, in fifty years it could happen again—two families not quite speaking and neither knowing exactly why.

ON CHRISTMAS IN ENGLAND, IT RAINS.

(Every day in England, it rains.)

My mother's cousin drives us from one end of London to the other, to my father's cousin's house, where we will stay the night before going to France. We are late; we stayed too long at one party before coming to this one. When we pull up in front of the house, it is bright with cars coming and going. My father's cousin is throwing the party for him, so that he can see all of his relatives at once. My father stumbles from the car, his eagerness as apparent as a child's. I have never seen him look like this.

Uncertain, he moves through the door and then into the hallway of the house, into the light room where almost every British relative he has is waiting for him. Almost fifty people here, I would guess. My mother—who unlike him is always sure of herself—is behind him. After her, me, watching my father and myself. It is like coming into another planet, the dance of sociality performed once more. We present our faces to the cousin we have never met and shake hands with her children, who are stunningly attractive.

We eat slowly. There is row upon row of pies, cheesecakes, rice, curries. We eat and watch my father, who is uncomfortable being the center of attention. I drift into a daze of conversation between my mother and the women around her. She shows me off to one female relative after another. They talk about me in the third person. I am not there. They are not being rude; this is how things are done. The elders compare their prizes, their children; how well you have done is shown in your children. I am especially intriguing to this branch of the family, having not been to England in nearly a decade. They remember me as a thin, bespectacled, bookish girl, with extremely long hair. Nearly more hair than girl, as Uma had once been. Now my mother presents me as I am: shorn and coltish, but an adult.

What are you studying?

English.

What does that lead you to?

I might be a doctor. I don't know. (In America you don't have to know.)

Oh. They nod at one another knowingly. In America, uncertainty is permitted. I suppress a sigh, glad that my father's long-ago visa application to the United Kingdom was denied. They smile at me approvingly. It is not a false approval. It is an expected approval.

What happens next is entirely unexpected. One moment all is lighthearted chatter. The next, two men are fighting each other at the other end of the room. As drunk as they might have been in Jaffna, but with fewer reasons. Two children run screaming back to their mother and she gathers them up. Two women—later, I realize they were twins—are trying to hold the men back. The other guests are frozen. One of the men fights the woman holding him, pushing her back, manipulating himself around until he is within arm's reach of a table. I see my father's lowering brow, his six feet moving across the room swiftly. I see that the man is reaching for an empty wine bottle. He raises his arm over his head, trying to move the woman aside, rearing back like an angry horse, bottle poised to crash down on his opponent's head. Another man shoulders between the furious men until the moment cools. None of us knows what they were fighting about. My eyes meet my father's, his horrified face mirroring mine: *this too is family.* On the left, my mother's posture has turned to marble. My gentle father looks shell-shocked. Transported temporarily back into the realm of his youth, he had forgotten the passions it held.

THAT ROOM WAS FILLED with people who wanted to embrace me. But I did not know any of them. Later my father identified them for me: a favorite aunt, a cousin who went to school with him, his second cousin's brother-in-law. I lose myself in names. In America, these names would stun people. Here in London, with its comfortable community of Sri Lankans and other South Asians, these names are like wine, better with age, silky, rolling off the tongue. *Yogamani. Balasubramanian. Jeyalakshmi.* If I had grown up in this sea of names, this colonial extension, I might have been like these people, who are comfortable with themselves and one another.

My parents named me *Yalini.* It means "music of Jaffna." I do not remember Jaffna, but I know that it is a place of ancient days and holy verses. A place to which I cannot go back.

I HAVE DINNER WITH my family together the night before Janani's wedding, which I have come to think of in the same way as a funeral. I thought that after this, we would never see one another. We would not miss one another, either. But we were family. And we owed one another this: one last night together in the house where her father had died and loved us both, so differently.

What is left of a family: Murali, Vani, Janani, Yalini. We invite Lucky and Rajie, because they have acted like our relatives, and because their presence honors my late uncle, whom we buried not so long ago. We sit around the table, eating a vegetarian meal, because that is the auspicious thing to do. None of us, even and perhaps especially Janani, knows Suthan any better than we did the first day we met him. What does he stand for? Who is she marrying?

I think at her: *You don't have to do this.* But I do not say it.

And I am not wrong. As my mother is serving out the rice, a Tamil man whose interests in Toronto rival Suthan's is walking up to the locked doors of the Tamil community center with bolt cutters. He is a tall man, about Suthan's age and height; he has a darker face, and a full beard, but he is skinny, and he wears similar black clothing. He has waited for darkness. Four other men flank him.

My mother serves the potato curry, placing a generous, saffron-laden mound next to each white pillow of rice, and the man enters the building, and with four quick gestures of his hand, dispatches his friends to the corners of the building, to make sure that there is no one in it. They are not looking to kill anyone. No one starts out that way, after all. As my father asks for another helping of coconut *sambol*, the man is playing a flashlight across the walls of the main room, its decorations, its map of Sri Lanka, its Hindu gods. He has donned leather gloves, his expression unreadable. He could be doing this in another country entirely. He pours gasoline all over the rugs, and all over the wooden frame of the *mānavarai*, the wedding altar Suthan has built for Janani, and which tomorrow would have been adorned with flowers.

My mother is making after-dinner tea and serving *vattalappam* for dessert, and the men are searching the rooms for valuables and locking down most of the windows, making sure the curtains are soaked in oil. As we bid Lucky and Rajie good-bye, the man is going up the stairs, into the rooms where Suthan has left Janani's *kūrai* sari, the sari of Wedding-Red silk, which he has planned to present to her during the wedding ceremony. The stranger picks the sari up and smells its newness; he spreads it out and admires the ornate *pallu*, the part that would fall over her shoulder. In his way he is a traditional man. What he is doing is part of tradition.

He puts the sari down, and my mother offers my father another cup of tea. He declines it, and the man puts on a ski mask and walks down the stairs from the second floor, back to the first. He leaves a trail of gasoline. Later, I will think of Rajie outside the take-out place, pointing out the places where one Tamil has shot another, for nothing. I help my mother put the curries away, and he closes the door behind him, removes the cut bolt, and walks away. I let Janani go to bed on her last night as an Un-Married woman, and the man gets into a car about a block away from the building. I am washing my face, and he is still looking back at the building. He starts the car and circles back to bring it to the front, where he pauses for his friends, who come out of the building's side doors and get in. He pulls four bottles up from near his feet. They are filled with gasoline and sugar—uncomplicated ingredients. And each bottle has an oiled rag dangling from its mouth, held in place by a cork.

As I walk up the stairs to go to bed, I do not hear a sound. The house is absolutely still and dark now, the strained sounds of my uncle's breathing gone. The man in the car pulls matches from his pocket and strikes one against his teeth, lighting each rag in turn. The house is quiet. Miles away, in a place empty of people, the stranger hands two flaming bottles to the men behind him. They roll their windows down, and the man in the driver's seat counts to three. Like twinned shooting stars, the bottles spiral through the air. Two, and then another two, the first pair shattering the hall's front windows.

The building lights up gradually at first. These are simple people; no C-4, no detonators, no complexity of wires. But still a spark paints a stripe down a trail of gasoline, to another, to another, until a web of light tightens like a fist around the structure in which Janani was to be Married.

We are in a different country, a different time.

But the building explodes.

It explodes.

It explodes.

SUTHAN: HE IS UNSURPRISED, and that is perhaps the most terrifying of all. When I wake up the next morning, I hear him talking downstairs, faster and more urgently than I have ever heard him speak before. I listen harder and realize I do not hear his father. He is here himself. His own man. I go downstairs, where he is talking to my father and to Janani. I hear the words *explosion* and *arson* and *gone.*

What?

Suthan looks at me, the intruder. Someone has burned down the community center, he explains.

What will you do?

Janani looks at my father. He looks back at her: it's her decision, not his. It was never his decision, or this whole wedding would not be happening.

We are still getting Married, Suthan says, his face harder and stronger for having to fight. At the temple, instead. Still today. No delays.

This is not a noble fight. It has nothing to do with the people dying in another country. It has to do with territory here, territory now, in this Western city. It's as Rajie said: no one is selfless. People profit off this war. In Sri Lanka, they do it by selling arms and feeding the black market. Here it's something different.

I look at Janani; my father looks at Janani. Suthan tilts his head down at her expectantly.

She pauses. She looks unhurried, as though she has all the time in the world and no one is waiting to know what she thinks. And then slowly, she begins to nod.

Yes, she says. Yes.

KUMARAN: IN MY HEAD, I am always burying my uncle. He died here, in Toronto, and his funeral was like an affair of state, the Tamil state that exists here, an island away from the island that we all remember. Even I remember that nation. And that is because of him. That is because I was raised in a house that could not forget it. A house where I was taught a language and a code that told me about an unofficial war. As a child I read about Tamils murdered, and a Tamil library burned. I knew a woman who, while watching the news, had seen her own mother blown up live on television. I heard stories about Tamils disappearing, Tamils tortured, Tamils killing Tamils. I learned a certain vocabulary. I learned to believe that a government could kill its own and drive them to commit unspeakable crimes. That no one would be right, but that some would be more wrong. I could hate Kumaran and still love him.

His body was burned here, in Toronto, and he had no son to light the pyre. My father did it. And when he died, finally Janani and I had something in common: even though she did not tell me, I knew that she was doing the same thing I was doing. We buried him in Jaffna. She knew the rituals of her funeral, and I dreamed mine, but we both burned him there. I do it again today, for the occasion of her Wedding: if there had never been a war, Jaffna is where he would have wanted to die.

IT IS AT MY COUSIN JANANI'S *kalyānam*, her wedding, that I first truly see and learn the Hindu rites of marriage. It is the first wedding in my generation of the family. I watch what transpires, wondering all the while if I will ever stand where Janani stands today, in an Arranged Marriage or a Love Marriage: wearing Wedding-Red. I am younger than she in more ways than one, although in true time, she has fewer years than I.

Because neither my mother nor I trusts my sense of Sri Lankan dress and propriety, she drapes my sari for me, as she did in the fittings. I have lost weight since she sewed the blouse, and my arms hang loosely in the sleeves, which according to fashion should be tight. I wear my grandmother Tharshi's earrings. My mother pronounces me dressed only after she dips her little finger in black *pottu* and anoints me with this paste, which is used to mark the foreheads of UnMarried Women. In Sri Lanka, this is done every day. My mother continues this custom, wearing the Wedding-Red mark of Married Women every morning. I only wear *pottu* for Weddings.

All my life, my mother has been my teacher. This is also true in the temple. My mother has taught me that a Hindu temple is very clean. As in most Hindu households, you must remove your shoes before entering and wash your feet. She reminds me that when I sit on the ground I must keep my legs crossed and make sure that I do not disrespect the gods by pointing my feet toward them. Do you have your period? Remember, if you have your menses the priests will not allow you inside the temple.

Now, as my cousin Janani is getting Married, is only my third or fourth time inside a real temple. The temple near our house was just being built when I was growing up. Hindus traveled far away to be married, and we worshipped the gods in a house on the temple site, which we treated as a real temple nonetheless. The priests came from India and wore only white cloths knotted around their waists. They tied threads of saffron around their hands and ankles for luck. They washed the gods and dressed them in silk. They offered them milk, honey, and yogurt. They marked them in bright colors: red, but also the holy ash called *viphuti*, which smells sweet, and saffron that had been turned into a paste. When they were done anointing the gods, we also wore these colors of worship. Most of the priests did not speak English, and so I did not talk to them. When I did not understand what was happening, I asked my mother. When we prayed I knelt beside or behind her and imitated her. I stood when she stood, clasped my hands together when she did, blessed myself with the holy fire that the priest held when she did.

I remember that during one special ceremony, my mother and I walked with a group of women behind the men, who carried an elaborate gold litter with one of the gods in it. I asked my mother why we could not carry the litter. She shook her head, her eyes still on the litter moving on the men's shoulders. There are no women priests, she said. Women have never carried the gods.

The house held all the gods for the temple, including the nine planets. My mother taught me that in prayer, we circle these nine deities. We each have a *natśattiram*, which is the star of birth. She taught me that at a certain point, in a certain prayer, the priest asks what my star is. I am *swāthi*. If I am ever Married, I will have to remember this. If my parents are superstitious, they will ask an astrologer to see if my star aligns with the star of my intended.

The most sacred place in a wedding ceremony is called the *mānavarai*. It is the altar. It is adorned with flowers, and it faces East, where the sun rises. In America the ceremony is strange enough to us that at weddings, guides explaining its different stages are passed out. The wedding guide takes us through the wedding ritual from beginning to end.

The priest recites the names of the forefathers of both bride and groom and asks for their blessings. My father had said that in Sri Lanka, a person did not bear his ancestors all his life. This is almost true. They appear only at the beginning and the end. As you come out of the island, and as you return to it. And as you are Married.

WHEN JANANI TOLD ME that she actually wanted to get Married, at first I did not believe her or understand. It was March, right before her father died. We were sitting out in the cold, gray yard. He had stopped taking walks there mostly. My father gave him pain medication four or five times a day.

I want to get married here, she said. It will make part of what is going on there, forever.

You are a part of it anyway, I said.

She did not believe me.

Her father died in April, just as blades of green were beginning to rise out of the gray garden behind that strange house. The house did not belong to us, and yet we had done so many personal things there. It had begun to feel like a home. We had sat vigil together at his bedside and cooked him meals in that kitchen. We had slept in those beds, and he had died there. That, of course, was the most personal thing. I know that some people do not want to be in houses where people they have loved have died, but I did not want to leave that house. It was the only place where I had known him. I thought that if I walked out the door and into Canadian spring sunshine it would feel like a world in which he had never existed.

But it was worse for her. It had to have been worse for her, because he was her father. I am guessing when I say this; she did not talk to me. And I was born lucky: I still have my father, and he is an exceptional man. I knew that she grieved not only for her father's passing, but for where and how it had taken place. This was still not her country, and yet he had moved into it so easily and died here. He had shown an ability to adapt that should have surprised no one and instead surprised everyone. I knew that she had sometimes listened at the door as my uncle talked to me, telling me about his life, and I wondered if she already knew what he was telling me, or if she just resented it. She too had been educated as a radical, but her education had been different from his, because she had grown up inside the movement and possibly still believed in it. And her father was not just telling me about politics. He was telling me about Meenakshi, whom she had never known, and Justine, who was from another world, that she did not know. She had never seen a white person before leaving Sri Lanka. The variety of her father's loves dismayed her, I think, whether she already knew of them or not. She wanted him to love the few things that she already knew: she resented his frankness with me, perhaps because she did not know why he felt he owed me anything. She had never had to share him.

Janani is very angry with me, he said to me on one of his last days. It was true that although she had gone into his room and spent more time there as the months wore on, she did not seem to speak. Even if it was only the two of them in there and I passed by outside, I heard nothing. Little conversation. Occasionally, a little bit of Tamil: *Appa*, do you need some water? Sometimes my father went in to check on him. He would carry in a small mug of water and a few pills, and my uncle would swallow them with great effort. Often he had a headache and would ask me to draw the curtains to block out the dull light off the snow. But he almost never stopped talking.

My daughter hates me because I have decided what I think, he said. But you don't hate me, even though I've sacrificed your independence by being here.

You're only here for a short while, I said to him. I'm hardly giving up my independence.

His eyes widened in alarm. Oh, no, he said. You don't understand. They told me when I came here that they were permitting this because of the family's loyalty. I gave them a promise. You know that the Tigers have supporters here. It was a trade—I came here, and you and your mother and your father are expected to toe the line. You don't have to do anything dramatic. But you can't really speak against them. Not here.

I didn't promise them anything, I said.

Sometimes promises can be made for you, he said. Sometimes in life things don't work out as smoothly as we'd like. It doesn't matter what you say when you're walking around. Say what you have to say to be safe. You can still decide what you believe and say that to yourself.

If someone had said that to you back when you were joining the Tigers you would have disagreed with them, I said. Of course it matters what you do. I can't think something and act in another way.

Not even to save yourself or your parents from a certain degree of pain?

In my memory, he is still saying this, and I am still shaking my head, unable to agree with him. Although I know that the reason Janani's face is blank and cold is because she has not yet accustomed herself to the idea of a future.

IN APRIL, BEFORE HE DIED, WHEN IT became clear that the cold was over, my uncle's face began to change even more. His headaches became more frequent. One day, when I was in the kitchen washing dishes, I looked out the window over the sink and back into the gray garden. I saw him fall and shake. His eyes rolled up into his head and my mother screamed. I could hear her scream even through the glass and I raced upstairs to get my father. He ran down the stairs and outside, grabbing a towel from the kitchen on the way. I thought I had heard something once about making sure seizure victims did not swallow their own tongues, but my own tongue did not seem to work properly. My father did put the towel into Kumaran's mouth, bracing himself against my uncle's shoulders to try to get him to stop seizing.

Watching them, I felt bile rise up in my throat and pushed it back. Two men, both old and getting older, one healthy and hale, one dying. At the beginning it was supposed to be the other way around. The seizure lasted only a few minutes, but it was briefly and intensely terrifying. Janani came up behind me and looked out the window too, and her face scared me even more because it was so blank.

This used to happen all the time at home, she said. This is how they first knew he was sick. This and the headaches.

That was scary, but worse was his voice, because it took me so long to notice it vanishing. It gradually slid away and out of his control. On some days he could speak with great clarity and lucidity, but sometimes he would retell me a story he had told me before, but with different times or people. Sometimes the events changed. His eyes turned inward, as though they saw nothing before them. His face changed. And so did my own as I watched him.

I WAS BORN LUCKY: I grew up safe and warm. No governments sent soldiers to move into my village. I did not worry about my house burning or my pictures being lost. I did not worry about dying. I did not fear having too little to eat. I never stood on queue for a ration of rice or slept in a temple for refuge. I lived in a place of plenty. I had so much to eat that as I watched my uncle die, I began to forget to do so. Watching his face transform, I learned to hate mirrors for the health they reflected. This was not the same hatred that Kunju had for her reflection after her accident. Kunju is long dead, and I never met her. My revulsion at my own image was something I learned, not something that happened to me suddenly, like the fire that took her face from her.

This happened to me little by little, morning by morning, like droplets of water gathering to form a pool. And I drank that water willingly and took its poison into myself. I am someone who watched my own face change very carefully. I am familiar with the planes and angles of my own geography. I know each scar and irregularity. In that house in Scarborough, I sometimes woke up in the middle of the night and went to the glass to see if my face still looked the same. I stared into my own eyes, barely a finger's width from my mirrorself. No distance. I measured the space between my eyes, the length of my nose, the width of my forehead, the shape of my mouth.

My uncle was disappearing. And my own reflection seemed all wrong. There was too much of me, and the spaces between my parts were not in proportion to one another. My stomach was not acquainted with my hips. In listening to my uncle and my father and even my mother, I had become a stranger to myself. I did not know how to see myself next to these people. As my father once imagined that his Heart was too weak and too big, I looked into the mirror and saw a body grown oceanic.

I woke up every morning wondering what would happen,

what death would look like when it came. One morning my uncle woke up wanting a mango, and we lived in Scarborough, Toronto, where a mango was not a dying man's dream, but a wish that could be fulfilled. My father sent Janani and me into the city to find the fruit, and also to buy the few small items that my mother might want to decorate the small household shrine.

When we passed shop windows together as we walked down the street, I looked away. She was so much smaller than I. She was dainty and fine-boned. Next to her I looked clumsy and uncomfortable in my own skin. *Which I was.* My mother had defeated biology. In a family of women with generous bodies, she was thinner, and thinner, and thinner still. Yet she moved with a life I did not have. When I was alone in my room I stripped down and measured the space between my shoulders. I held my belly and pinched its excess. My hips and my thighs were broad. I was twenty-two. It is an age at which some women are Married. This includes the women in my family.

You want to hear something I liked about myself? My teeth are perfect. My mother told me to smile with them showing. But when I finally really understood that my uncle was dying, when I slept, I clenched my teeth and ground them. When I woke my jaw ached. Even as a child, I had trouble sleeping. Even in that house in Canada, I still slept with a light on. When I was small, I tossed and turned so restlessly that my parents put rails on my bed, so that I would not fall out of it. Even so, some mornings, they found me sprawled on the floor. When I woke up in the middle of the night, I had to pass the household shrine to get a glass of water. I was sure that the eyes of the gods moved, following me as I walked across the hall. Many-armed Lakshmi looking at me. I held my breath as I passed them, the way that superstitious Americans hold their breath when passing cemeteries. In the years since, this became unconscious and constant. I held my breath in class, in my sleep, in conversations. My mother sometimes asked me why I was holding my breath. What was I waiting for? What was I so afraid of not finishing? I was being watched. The gods were watching me, and they did not approve. I bathed only in very hot water, letting rivulets of water run down my body for so long that my mother knocked to ask if I was all right. This steamed up the mirror so that when I stepped out, I was not faced with the macabre view of that distorted reflection.

If a stray lock of hair on my head bothered me I ripped or cut it off. There was a patch of very short hair in the middle of my scalp, across the part, where it started to grow back. Like Harini's bare spot, behind her ear, except that I did this to myself, and it grew back. In sleep or daydreams I scratched at my imperfections until I bled. Sometimes I woke to find the sheets smeared with red. I scarred easily and so I bore the scars of my fear. I washed my hands every hour, scared to think of what had touched me, or what I had touched. Sometimes I thought if I stood under the water long enough, I could wash away all the dangerous parts of myself. The longer I knew my uncle and my cousin, the more of these parts there were. I wished that my Heart was too big; I wished it could absorb the rest of my body so that no one could see me. There is a trick, you see, to being a scientist, to writing about myself in the first person. You must write about your pain without subscribing to the theory that you need sympathy. *Why are you writing that down? Don't keep a grudge against yourself.* I will not keep the grudge. I am only recording it. I am writing because I want to know what happened to me. How I started to disappear, even though I had everything that Kunju, Tharshi, Mayuri, Harini, and Uma did not. Sometimes I cried and could not stop. Sometimes I laughed and could not stop. I traveled into darkness and madness, as Uma did before me. As a child, I lulled myself to sleep by listening to the sound of my own voice inside my mind. Now I tried to shut out all sounds, even that sound, the beloved sharp and sweet of the story. Because I did not want to hear what my uncle was truly saying between his words. Burning oneself is called immolation, and in some places it is a holy act. When Hindus die, our bodies are burned on a funeral pyre. Someone we have loved is asked to light the torch. For a long time, many people asked that their ashes be scattered in the holy river Ganges. Pilgrims bathe in this same water to sanctify themselves.

If I had had the courage, I would have set myself on fire, which would have been bright and would have burned away the darkness. This was not Uma's darkness. It was a different darkness, because it was a darkness that could be stopped.

KUMARAN: THE LAST TIME I talked to my uncle before he died. He asked to see me alone. I went to his room in that cold Scarborough house and closed the door. It was cold. He lay there, holding his head. This was, of late, his position. He said:

If you have any questions left you had better ask them.

I shrugged.

About families? About ours? Well? he said, impatient. Ask them. I'll be gone, you know.

I think you're a liar, I said. I already asked you questions. You told me all sorts of things, you told me about your life, and you said you were not prejudiced.

I'm not.

I just don't know why I should believe anything you say. You confessed twenty-five years late. You told me what you tried to do to my father, and you thought that by that confession alone, I would understand how you felt and what could make you do that?

Do you think people don't change? my uncle said. I know that what your father did for your mother was better than anything anyone else could have done. If he had told her where I was, she would have come back to Sri Lanka. Or she would have tried to find me, somehow. That would have been very dangerous, from any standpoint. The army would have suspected her of collusion. She might have disappeared or been killed. You wouldn't be here.

I sat back in the chair next to his bed. The vinyl stuck to my back.

You wouldn't be here, I said.

I killed people, he said. Do you know that? That when I was a child, I ate every meal with your mother, and then I grew up and I killed people? I trained to kill people. Sometimes I even liked it. And your mother still wanted to find me.

He was trying to shock me into hearing him, and I didn't want to be shocked. Who did you kill? I asked. You left that out of the story when you were telling me about your family. I was working to keep my voice flat and uninterested, but I was interested.

I killed the woman I was supposed to marry, he said. Not Janani's mother. That was my fault too, but in a different way. I should have protected the mother of my child. But the first woman—her name was Meenakshi.

I know about her, I said. You told me about that. You didn't do that. It was a suicide bomber.

I did it, he said, because I was part of the movement. Do you know what they do to people who disagree with them? You have to let me take responsibility. If you don't forgive me, what happens if the war ends? You just throw out all the people who did wrong? Do you know how many people that is? Almost everyone, Yalini. Almost everyone.

KUMARAN HAD GROWN UP with my mother, and I could see how happy she was to see him, how happy she was that he had chosen to spend his last days with us, and not on war. I looked at her and I thought, *She doesn't know, does she? She hasn't ever seen that letter.* That letter, in which Kumaran hinted that if my father planned a wedding for Vani, someone in his family would be dead inside a month. Because he was not good enough for her.

By the time my father proposed to my mother, you see, Kumaran had already disappeared. He had joined the Tigers, who he thought shared his notions of radicalism. Equality. And then he heard about Vani's engagement probably through another Tiger cadre, a fellow from Ariyalai who had been home and whose family knew my father's.

It was only when he actually crashed through that door in Neelan's house, bearing a Tiger threat, that he realized what a hypocrite he was. He hated himself, just as later I would hate him. He forgave himself, just as much later, too late, I would forgive him. He emerged from anonymity for a forbidden moment, and my father did not tell my mother about it. Although he knew—roughly—where Kumaran was and she did not.

That was a long time ago, my uncle said.

I love my father, I said.

As Janani loves her father, he said. Look at what she's doing. She knows that she cannot go back, and this is the next best thing she can think of. Do you think that will do anyone any good, if it isn't what she truly wants?

I thought about that for a long time after he died. *Look at what she's doing.* I am not close to Janani. Why was she getting married in this fashion? And then I realized what he meant. She was doing it for him, because she thought he would want to see tradition preserved, if not in the form of a Tamil country, then in the form of a Tamil daughter.

MY COUSIN JANANI IS GETTING MARRIED. To my eye she looks very thin and lovely. Her hair is long and wavy. Today it is braided with flowers and gold. Her lips and cheeks have been reddened. Her eyes are heavily outlined with dramatic dark smudges. When she arrived in Canada, we looked alike. Now, standing next to her, I see no resemblance between us.

After she is Married, her brow will be marked with a red circle, like my mother's. Today, Janani is a goddess: the ceremony itself is conducted so that the groom represents the god Shiva, and his wife-to-be plays the part of Shiva's consort, Parvati. Shiva is also called the Destroyer. This is how the ceremony begins.

The Bridegroom's Welcome: When the groom arrives at the ceremony, the bride's parents greet him formally. The *tōli*, a female related to the groom, brings the *tāli*, the wedding necklace, and the *kūrai* to the wedding. The *tāli* is the gold chain that binds the bride to the groom in purity. The *kūrai* is the Wedding-Red sari that the bridegroom has chosen for his intended. All my life I have seen this sari in pictures and old homemade films. This Red that is so desired.

The bridegroom arrives and comes to the *mānavarai*. In the background I can hear the *nātasaram* beginning: the holy music that can be heard throughout the ceremony, just under the priest's words. Even my mother cannot translate what he is reciting. It is language far older than even Tamil: Sanskrit.

ON ONE DAY DURING this time after Kumaran's death and before Janani's Wedding I stopped recording what he had said. About himself. About anything. My Heart remembered Kunju's rage at her own face. I take this rage and multiply it and make it my own. I put it in my Heart to keep it warm and bank its fire. I am angry at what my uncle Kumaran did, and I am angry that he is gone.

I think Hindu weddings are so long because there are so many rituals for protection and to cast away evil. Getting Married means that you are passing a milestone in the evolution of your soul. As they are married, the bride and groom sit higher than the congregation, on par with the gods. I think that this must be a view from which everything else seems smaller. I think this must be dangerous. I think my soul could not stand such an evolution. I do not know how to be touched or purified. *Punyathānam*, which is purification: this is the first part of the wedding ceremony, and something that is done separately to the bride and to the groom, who are edging ever closer to sharing a life. The priest splashes the wedding place with holy water and asks for the blessing of the god Ganesha. A group of women perform the *pallikai kattu*, a ritual that removes any evil. How could I ever do this? This darkness feels irrevocable, untouched by these rituals.

The bridegroom's consent is sealed by the *tarppai*, a blade of sacred grass that is tied around his finger. This is *sangalppam*: the statement of intent. Another thread that has been blessed and colored saffron is knotted around his wrist. This is *kāpu kuttu*, also to protect against evil. After the bridegroom leaves the *mānavarai*, Janani arrives, and she is sanctified in the same way. I have never seen such a saffron thread on the wrist of anyone UnMarried, excepting a priest. The Ceremony's Heart: the groom returns and sits with Janani. He on the left, she on the right. The priest recites the prayers of Shiva-Parvati and Navagraha. This will protect them from the cosmic pull of the nine planets. In many cultures, we blame the occurrence of evil on the whims of the planets. I should know better than to do this, but like my family, I find myself believing.

Homām, the sacred fire, is lit. Then: the *dhanikka dhanam*, which is performed by Janani's uncle in lieu of her late father. My father places Janani's right hand into the groom's. Into these entwined hands he places a gold coin and other symbols of a prosperous life. The priest announces their names, and the names of their forefathers and mothers, going back in their families three generations. He asks for the blessings of all those present and living, all those present in spirit, and, lastly, Agni, the god of fire. It is Agni who serves as the voice between heaven and earth. He is a god of the otherworld.

Based on what I know of him, I think Agni must be an angry god. But Janani is smiling.

KUMARAN AND I ARE, after all, not so different. We both tried to stop weddings, and both of us failed. Look at what she's doing, he had said.

Janani, I said tentatively. I want to ask you about something your father said before he died.

My father, she said. Go ahead.

He said that you were—he implied, really—that you were getting Married for him. Not because you wanted to. Because this kind of Marriage is what you thought he wanted for you.

She laughed. Is that what he said?

Is this really what you want? I asked.

Yes, she said. It is. And you don't have any choice but to believe me.

You don't have to do this, I said. You could still call it off. No one would be angry.

Yes, I do, she said. Don't you see? I know what he tried to do to your parents. But this is what I want, just like that was what they wanted. I know that my father said all sorts of things to try to stop their wedding—that your father wasn't good enough, that he wasn't rich or successful. That he could have your father killed. I think he was bluffing. But it doesn't matter. When your father got that letter, do you know what he wrote back? He wrote a letter that said *go ahead and try.* He knew that no one who loved your mother could do that, if he was really what she wanted. This is what I really want.

I didn't have anything to say to that.

She stepped back to look at me carefully. Listen to me, Yalini: my father wasn't trying to get you to stop my wedding. He was trying to show you that it couldn't be done, because it's what I want. It's meant to happen because I chose it. Like your mother chose your father. I'm choosing Suthan and in choosing Suthan, I'm choosing a cause.

You can be against this if you want—this type of Marriage. But keep in mind that most people are not like your parents. This is a tradition of the place where I was raised, and where by rights you should have been raised. If you try to talk me out of it because you think it's not what I want, you're being too simple. Look at how far you already are from everything Sri Lankan. That's how you see yourself, but that's not how others will see you.

You cannot just opt out, she said. You have to choose.

AFTER MY UNCLE DIED, I returned to school. I went back to a campus now mostly empty of my classmates, who had graduated and moved on. My friend, whom I had cut off after the tsunami, had left. I did not know where he was, and it did not matter, because Kumaran had erased the person whom he had known. Still, sometimes I would remember that friend and start across the street, or down a library corridor, thinking that I had seen him. But I was alone with myself again, and myself was someone different.

Now, some months after Kumaran's death, we are back in Scarborough, Toronto, the home of many Tamils, with many opinions about what they do, and what has been done to them. No law makes me accountable to them but the laws of ancestry and society. I am not accountable to anyone, but I am afraid and my fear spins out of my control. But this is not about a body: not my father's once frail Heart grown strong, or my uncle's brain and its cancer consuming him. It is not about my body and its ease of survival. It is about deciding what I think of what my uncle did, the promise that he made on behalf of our family in the West, so that he could die Here and not There. If he can be forgiven, and where I stand on the shifting ground of war. A noncombatant, but complicit nonetheless if I am silent.

I know that while it may not matter yet, one day, soon, it will. People will want to know. I want to know myself. Where do I stand? I envy Janani's certainty. She has shifted countries, but not positions. The man the Tigers found for her, the man walking around the fire with her, may match her. He is not afraid of the things that she did as a young woman growing up in the movement, things that she had never told me, but that I suspect. He is able to dream the two of them into new selves, living in a happier Sri Lanka. That happier Sri Lanka does not exist, but his faith impresses her. To tell the truth, it impresses me too.

I envy it, this faith. I wanted to be certain of my convictions.

I knew that there were people whose loved ones had died at the hands of the Tigers, and I wondered what they thought of people like my uncle, whose loved ones had died at the hands of the government. I wondered how and if they chose to be like him, or not like him.

Sometimes I too dream myself into another self. As a child when I was daydreaming I would look at my palms and then turn my hands over quickly to see if they had changed color. Everyone's palms are the same color. The backs of our hands betray us for the colors we truly are. My dream is like this: I turn my ankle, and my knee, and my hip, and my ribs, and my neck. I reach inside and twist my Heart, my lungs. I turn myself inside out and find that I am a person of color even inside. Some people would try to put a name to that color, to call it the name of a tree or a spice. I hate very little, but this is a thing that I hate. I cannot do this. I cannot name my own color.

My father sees this. He sees all of this. He sees that I love my mother enough to want to be exactly like her, even down to her unequivocal love of her brother, and to not understand why I cannot. As he once saw how her generous face would be sharpened and honed down to only what was necessary, he sees how I have placed myself into a sphere in which I do not belong. Uma's otherworld. My uncle told me that it did not matter what I said—only what I believe.

My face in the mirror mocks its earlier innocence. I still cannot tell you everything my uncle did. I do not want to know. I learned to love him and I do not know or want to know what he did. Who he killed. Although these things are a part of him. If I am willing to imagine another self, then I have to know that the things he did, the things that Janani did—these are things I could have done. I knew him well enough to know: governments call men terrorists to erase their reason, to make them crazy. Some of them are, and some of them are not. What does that make me?

MY FATHER WATCHES ME. Am I his Heart? He remembers how as a child they listened to his chest and told him he would die. It is possible he is remembering his sister, but I think he is hoping I turn out like his Heart. Healed, after all. Still beating, despite what was said.

KUMARAN: HE WOULD HAVE been impressed, I think, with how his son-in-law received the nearest Hindu temple's permission to be Married the same day, in their courtyard. How all the guests moved without comment, how my mother acquired a new *kūrai* sari as a gift from the sari shop owner. The sun and the gods shone brightly on his daughter. I watched her, and in my head, I let him go.

I had to study how to do this, because his was my first funeral. Both death and marriage require fire. If we were in Jaffna, having a funeral, the sons of the dead man would gather around an *ayer*, a priest, a Brahmin. The priest would give the *mutal makan*, the first son, a *tarppai* for the ring finger of his right hand. In following this custom, the first son becomes a Brahmin, who can partake in all the rituals of the funeral.

The *ayer* assembles vessels for the ceremony; in Tamil, he identifies them as Siva, Sakthi, and Ganesha. With these words, the body and soul of the deceased take on godlike qualities.

The *ayer* lights the fire. In the fire, he burns all the holy materials—*manjal*, sandalwood, and camphor. As they burn, they remove all the bad things in life: desire, jealousy, evil, harmful thoughts or intentions. The soul of the deceased travels through this to the place where only good things reside. There is no room for anything evil.

I have to believe this about my uncle now.

If he had had sons, if he had had male grandchildren, they would have ringed his body, going around him as he transformed into a god. They would be followed by the women.

They would carry the body outside the house to bathe it. The *dhobi*, the washerman, would assist in this. It would be done with great tenderness, with *arappu*, a seed from a certain kind of tree. It would be done with oil, with water, with cow's milk, with water from a coconut. It would be done with honey, and with curd.

First: the sons and grandsons would bathe him. But because my uncle had none, my father would have done it. And then Janani and I would have touched him, using the *tarppai* to smooth all this into his brow three times. We would have washed our right hands with water, and the men would have carried Kumaran back into the house, into the courtyard at the center of the house, where the Mourners would be waiting.

Any man can become a god like this. All you have to do is die, and Mourners will sing the *mānikka vasakam*, the verses of forgiveness. In the place of my uncle's unborn first son, my father would have circled the body thrice, bearing a garland. He would place the garland around my uncle's throat and rub ash and *kunkumum*, the red paste, onto his forehead. He is a god. The others would place cut flowers at his feet.

Manjal, lime, white powder, and *kunkumum* are ground together into a paste as the *ayer* sings through the verses of forgiveness. The paste is mixed with rose water, and my father covers Kumaran's eyes with it. The women give the body food for the last time—rice. Then the youngest children, the grandchildren he might have had, hold *nay pandam*, lit sticks, in a circle around the body, so that the soul can leave it.

The priest says, Don't cry.

The men carry the body out, leaving the women.

AT THE CREMATION SITE, Chemmani, the body is removed from its wooden coffin and placed onto the funeral pyre. And the men too offer the deceased some rice. My father, as the lighter of the pyre, would have done it last.

They would have removed any remaining jewels or gold from his body. The rings from his fingers, the chain from around his neck. Everything permanent has been removed. The priest recites a last prayer as the *nenjaam kattai*, the first funeral logs, are placed on top of the body, so that it does not rise up as it is being burned.

On his left shoulder, my father carries the vessel of funeral water: water and petrol with coconut and mango leaves on top. He carries a lit stick in his right hand. He travels around Kumaran's body three times, followed by the *dhobi*. A small hole is made in the vessel, so that the funeral water spills onto the body.

My father goes to the funeral pyre, to the end where Kumaran's face looks up, just above the pile of wood on his still chest. Without looking he lights it. Without looking he walks away. The mourners do not look back.

EARTH, FIRE, WATER, ETHER, and wind compose the body. The earth receives the body, which has burned in fire. The wind transports its ashes to flowing water. And the ether, the unknown, returns to the afterlife.

Afterward the mourners return for *kātārru*. They must remove all signs of the body. They place fruits, honey, *manjal*, rosewater, and rice in the places on the pyre where the head, the breast, and the feet of the person they loved lay first. My father circles the place where the body was. Thrice.

They throw the ashes into the water.

My father returns to the house of mourning and bathes. He has been fasting. As the lighter of a pyre, he is forbidden from the temple for one year. *Āñtu tivasam.*

We travel away from my uncle—my mother, my father, and I. It takes many days.

SELAVU: THE DAY AFTER THE FUNERAL. For the first time since the death, the house of the dead prepares food and feeds the village, the family, and friends. The meal is free of any meat, and those attending bring some of the ingredients—rice, vegetables, perhaps a coconut—as a sign of help for the house that has lost one of its own.

ETTU KALAKKIRATU: EIGHT DAYS AFTER the funeral, the house of the dead cooks all the food that he enjoyed the most. For my uncle: potato curry, *vadai*, *dosai*, coconut *sambol*—things that do not go together, but that he enjoyed. In Jaffna, my mother takes this food and puts it in a corner of the house, the place where his body rested as it was being prepared for the pyre. She has left a picture of him there.

And on this, the eighth day, he comes back and finds himself at a break in the road, with five paths from which to choose. My father holds a plate out to him, calls out to him three times, and leaves the plate there.

Without looking back, my father returns to the house.

ANTHIRATTI: SIXTEEN DAYS AFTER Kumaran died, in my head, I am still in Jaffna. We perform the funeral rites again, without the body. We remember him. We remember him. We remember him. We talk about him only with Love. Everything else—darkness, history, war—is gone. Burned away.

HER FATHER DIED AND BECAME A GOD. Godlike, in two countries. He has gone across a divide and changed forever. Janani too changes: the wedding guests bless the *kūrai*, which Suthan has chosen for her, and which is the most visible symbol of her transformation. The groom gives her the *kūrai*. He waits for her to return at the *mānavarai*. This is a conversational intermission in the ceremony, its slowest part. She is gone and everyone waits for her to come out.

When she returns, wearing Wedding-Red, it is the *mankalya dhāranam*. She does look different; if I saw her on the street, I am not sure I would recognize her. Her red lips and cheeks paint sharp angles on her pale face. Her lashes are very long, and she looks down demurely and properly. The priest hands the *tāli* to the groom, who ties it around Janani's throat. Like my mother, she will wear this all her life. In the background the priest chants prayers. Bells are rung. The wedding music rises, and they garland each other, shy hands skittering away from accidental contact of flesh to flesh. They are Married. They are Married. They are Married. When they sit back down in the embrace of the *mānavarai*, they have exchanged places and the groom sits on Janani's right. I move with the parade of girls through the sea of guests, passing food among them to celebrate the moment. I do this mechanically, my eyes fixed on my cousin.

The newlyweds, holding hands, walk three times around the sacred fire. Some of the most religious Hindus claim that they can walk on burning coals. I do not believe this; no one can walk in fire. If I ever wear Wedding-Red, I will make sure I walk around the fire, and not through it.

THE LAST PART OF THE wedding is the blessing. The bride and the groom have been cleansed spiritually. They have been given the guards against evil and the tokens that promise success. They have been tied to each other with the *tāli,* the chain. They have imitated the act of the gods Shiva and Parvati. The bride has promised her fidelity and her love. The groom has pledged his protection.

They return to the *mānavarai,* the ceremonial altar, which is adorned with flowers. Everyone who is present at the wedding throws blue grass and rice to ensure the pair's good fortune as they enter the world together.

Aratti: two women whom the couple loves bless them by passing a tray of lighted wicks back and forth before them. Then the guests line up to individually bless and honor the bride and the groom. This is the end of the ceremony. This is the beginning of the Marriage.

THIS IS AN ARRANGED MARRIAGE TOO, something ordained not by the stars, but by me: this meeting of girl and country. Single Sri Lankan Tamil girl. (Slim, educated, tall.) Born in the United States. Father is a doctor, mother is a teacher. (Sober habits.) I do not have to walk out of this country now to be safe. My parents did that for me, and that is an act of love too great for me to ever repeat. Some people leave their spouses for the sake of their children. My parents left a country for each other when they had not even met yet—for me, when I had not been born yet. Someday, I will be able to walk into that country again, because they walked out of it. When I do it will be a different place than the one they knew. But today it is a country held together by lies. Shells fall and no one claims them. People disappear and bereaved families bury no one.

In my memory, weddings are marked not by the fragrance of orange blossoms but by the dark scent of the fire, which is called the *homām.* Whereas for Kunju, fire meant an UnMarriage, and for Kalyani it meant the loss of her home. All my life, this has been the end of the film, the play, the story: She got Married. She lived happily ever after. This is not a straight lie, but rather a lie of omission. The story cannot always end in a marriage. Sometimes it goes beyond that. And sometimes we live our lives alone. This might be my future, but I have learned to live with what is mine and imperfect. I have learned that on some days, there is darkness so deep. Our lives begin without fanfare and end without warning.

Although they have traveled far, my parents and sometimes their families cannot help looking back with longing to the time when they knew the order of things. Their lives do not often surprise them. They were born, grew up, and got Married. I am not getting Married anytime soon, despite the speculative looks of my family, which is not quite sure or comfortable about what will happen to my generation. They do not like that there is no precedent for us—that some of us will not travel their path. We are not quite safe, and they would like to see the matter settled: we leave them with queasy stomachs and unsettled Hearts. But although we are the children of our parents, we have entered other countries in which the rules of Marriage—Love Marriage, Arranged Marriage, and all that lies in between—do not always apply.

Acknowledgments

A NUMBER OF PEOPLE HELPED AND SUPPORTED ME IN THE writing of this book.

In Sri Lanka:

I wish to thank those individuals and institutions that helped me with my research, most of whom—for their security—I have been advised not to name. They know who they are. Many of them went out of their way to talk to me and to help me find the books and materials I needed. I appreciate their assistance more than I can say.

I am particularly indebted to my traveling companions for my two most recent trips: my cousin Meera and her generous friends; and my father.

In America:

In Maryland—my teachers: Jan Bowman, Shellie Berman, Faith Roseman, Celia Harper, Wren Abramo, Suzanne Coker, and the late Renee Malden.

At Harvard College: the English department of 1998–2002, especially my first fiction professor, Patricia Powell—and, of course, my thesis adviser, Jamaica Kincaid, without whose encouragement I would never have begun *Love Marriage*, and whose particular brand of meticulous attention continues to be the standard for which I strive.

At the Iowa Writers' Workshop—my professors: the late, great Frank Conroy, Ethan Canin, James Hynes, Elizabeth McCracken, James McPherson, Chris Offutt, ZZ Packer, and Marilynne Robinson. I am grateful for the support of Lan Samantha Chang. Special thanks also to Connie Brothers. Deb West and Jan Zenisek make the Workshop not only run but feel like home. My classmates at Iowa, especially the women of salon. Elizabeth McCracken commented on an early version of this book, and the students of her fall 2003 novel class did the same. Special thanks also to Roderic Crooks, Yiyun Li, Tim O'Sullivan, Tracy Manaster, Jody Caldwell, and Becky Lehmann. Special thanks to English professor Miriam Gilbert.

At Phillips Exeter Academy: the English department of 2005–2006; and the George Bennett Fellowship, which gave me quite a bit more than a room of my own for a year. Elias Kulukundis, Charles and Joan Pratt, Maggie Dietz, and Todd Hearon. The students and faculty of Phillips Exeter, who love to read and to write. Julie Quinn and Michael Golay, kind neighbors; Vivian Komando; all my Exeter friends.

At Columbia University: Professor Alisa Solomon and my classmates in Arts and Culture. The students and professors of the MA program. Professor Samuel G. Freedman, whose guidance to a thesis topic indirectly influenced this novel. Professor D. Samuel Sudanandha, who taught me beginning Tamil. The graduate students studying Sri Lankan anthropology; the great Sri Lankan anthropologist E. Valentine Daniel. I wish particularly to note the help of Kitana Ananda, a new friend and a good one, who read a draft of this book. I am also especially grateful for the assistance of Mythri Jegathesan, my oldest friend, who read multiple drafts of this book and provided notes for the funeral ritual and helped me with transliterated words. I am incredibly indebted to you. (Any remaining errors are, of course, mine.) Ravindran Sriramachandran and Kaori Hatsumi, whose knowledge informed me and thus the book. Professor Sreenath Sreenivasan.

My Sri Lankan communities and relatives, who are, in fact, globe-scattered. My gratitude in particular to my friends and relatives in New York City; Connecticut; Maryland; Washington, D.C., and Lancaster, California; Toronto, Canada; Munich, Germany; Paris, France; Australia; and London, England.

My fellow artists in the Sri Lankan diaspora.

My friends: especially Michael Horn, Vicky Hallett, Stacy Erickson, and Matt MacInnis. Jonelle Lonergan, who set up my website.

The family Fallows, especially Jim and Tad.

Mathu Subramanian, a beautiful person and writer.

Kate Currie and Emily Halpern, both of whom read and commented on drafts of this book; and who lived with me when it was first being written. Joyce K. McIntyre, Ross Douthat, Abby Tucker, Catherine Cafferty, and James Renfro, who at various points all read and commented on drafts of this book.

Suketu Mehta. Photographer Preston Merchant.

My friends, past and present, at *The Harvard Crimson.*

My agent at the Gernert Company, Stephanie Cabot, who is always in my corner, and whose wisdom and ability to do it all astounds me. Chris Parris-Lamb, also of Gernert, upon whose keen eye I rely.

My friend of twenty-three years, who is also now my editor: Random House's Becca Shapiro. I am so lucky to have you as both; your suggestions strengthened this book immeasurably. What a pleasure to have someone with whom my intellectual and creative collaboration began in . . . kindergarten. The family Shapiro.

My sister-in-law, an inspiring woman. My inimitable and amazing brother. My parents: still the best people I know.

LOVE MARRIAGE

V. V. GANESHANANTHAN

A READER'S GUIDE

A conversation with

V. V. GANESHANANTHAN

Suketu Mehta is a fiction writer and journalist based in New York. He has won the Whiting Writers Award, the O. Henry Prize, and a New York Foundation for the Arts Fellowship for his fiction. He is the author of *Maximum City: Bombay Lost and Found*, and his other work has been published in the *New York Times Magazine, Granta, Harper's* magazine, *Time, Condé Nast Traveler*, and *The Village Voice* and has been featured on National Public Radio's *All Things Considered.*

Suketu Mehta: Sometimes people who go to Sri Lanka—I've gone there many times—throw up their hands and say you've got the most beautiful country in the world, but there are these two peoples who are just locked in what seems to be a suicidal senseless conflict. So talk a little bit about your impressions of the origin of the conflict and how it's affected your family and the family in the book.

V. V. Ganeshananthan: It took me a long time to understand anything about the origins of the conflict. I think that when you're a kid and your parents tell you a certain set of stories, and parts of those stories are true and maybe also parts of those stories are colored by their perspectives a little—which isn't to say what my parents told me wasn't true—but it wasn't exactly the only truth there was. So one of the things I did when I was researching the book was to read a whole bunch of books about Sri Lanka and to try and figure out exactly what historians thought was the defining truth.

One of the things people always talk about with regard to Sri Lanka is which people were there first. And I think that's a little bit besides the point, because both sets of people, the Tamils and the Sinhalese (who are not even the only two peoples involved in the conflict) really have been there for thousands of years. And then you have other populations: the Indian Tamils or the tea estate Tamils, and then also the Muslim population, which is Tamil-speaking, and you have Burghers, with their mixed European ancestry—so you really have a whole bunch of different populations. And I think if you're going to talk about who was there longest and that being the reason that you have a claim, then all over the world you've got big problems with the feasibility of restoring everyone to where they were first. It's not really a way to lay claim to land, necessarily.

SM: How long has the war been going on between the Tamils and the Sinhalese?

VG: I was reading online a story by one news agency, the AFP, that put the date at 1972, and the Associated Press, whose coverage I really admire, usually puts the date at 1983.

And 1983 is a pretty pivotal point in the book. The heroine is born in July 1983 and the war is usually dated to 1983 because of what was called Black July, which were anti-Tamil riots in the capital of Sri Lanka. And in which a great many Tamils were killed, and government officials and security forces did nothing, and in fact actually egged them on. So the war really took off after that. But the 1972 date that the AFP uses, there's an argument for that too. Certainly in the early 1970s . . . there was leftist thought going on all over the world, and the founders of the Tamil New Tigers, which later became the Tamil Tigers, they sort of started getting together in the early '70s, so there's a reasonable argument for that too, although it's a less common date.

So it's been going on for about twenty-five years by most people's count. But it's important to realize that like any war, it's the result of things that happened for decades before. The Sri Lankan government started discriminating against Tamils very shortly after the country gained independence from the British in the late 1940s. This has been well documented. The riots of 1958, for example. The war is really a culmination of previous events. It doesn't justify the Tigers' violence, but it does provide appropriate context.

SM: How many people have been killed in the conflict?

VG: To be honest it's hard to tell. The *New York Times* has covered this a little bit, and so have other organizations. A lot of people in Sri Lanka over the course of the war have simply disappeared. And so they never turn up or no one ever finds the bodies. So there are probably quite a few people who are dead and just no one knows where they are . . . And when so many people have been displaced it's very hard to take any sort of census. I think that one of the current numbers being tossed around is about seventy thousand.

SM: But that's still an amazing number in a country whose population is not even twenty million.

VG: Right. I think in the past couple of years there have been some four thousand people who have been killed or just disappeared. One thing that is very common right now in the north is for people to just be kidnapped. It's even happened a couple of times in the capital. People disappear into white vans, which have become this sign of rogue elements of who knows what, maybe it's the rebels, maybe it's the government, and people are kidnapped. Oftentimes it is Tamil civilians who are being kidnapped. And a lot of them have actually been journalists.

SM: Now, why has this conflict been allowed to go on for so long? A few years ago when I visited the country it seemed like there was peace everywhere, and everybody that I met in the north and the south agreed on the necessity for peace. That's all gone south, as it were. Why haven't any of the great powers stepped in and imposed a peace on the warring parties?

VG: I really wish they would. I think that's it's just unfortunately not economically necessarily important enough and I think also there's obviously the very hairy question of terrorism in the post 9/11 environment. The Tigers were identified by the Sri Lankan government, they were named terrorists way back, way back in the day, almost from their very origins. And Sri Lanka had a Prevention of Terrorism Act that was targeting that group and groups similar to it. But they're a military operation too . . . they're often—not always but often—targeting military targets . . .

But then other governments have a hard time telling the Sri Lankan government to negotiate with the Tigers, because the Tigers obviously have also engaged in other activities. They've attacked civilians, they use suicide bombers—they use tactics that are politically very touchy. Of course they're also dramatically outnumbered. I'm not saying that that justifies it—but they're a smaller force using rather extreme tactics, which then makes it hard for another government, the United States, for example, which has condemned terrorism, to say to the Sri Lankan government, Well, you should really be negotiating with this group to achieve some sort of peace. And of course the Tigers have also been responsible for killing a lot of Tamils who didn't agree with them.

SM: When did your family leave Sri Lanka, and what part of Sri Lanka do they come from?

VG: My parents are Ceylon Tamils, which means that my mother's *ūr* and my father's *ūr* are both in Jaffna. My parents came to the United States in the 1970s, and there was quite a wave of immigration then. That's very anecdotal, but my father, and my father's classmates from medical school, many of them emigrated around that time.

SM: How does the diaspora of the Sri Lankan Tamil community worldwide—there are a lot of them all over Europe and America—how do they carry on the memory of what has been lost? How do they deal with this not being able to return? My accountant is a Jaffna Tamil and he keeps describing a lost Eden . . .

VG: That's similar to how I feel about it, and I wasn't born there. It's interesting, in Toronto where the narrator is for most of the story, there are actually assemblies on Black July every year, and the Tigers were relatively recently declared terrorists in Canada, so it's become a little bit touchier to talk about which of their goals one might support even if one doesn't support their tactics. It becomes very politically complicated for people in the diaspora, and also, the diaspora has been criticized for funding the Tigers in a variety of ways because people overseas are making money that their kin in Sri Lanka are not. A lot of the diaspora, particularly in Canada, left Sri Lanka after 1983, and so they haven't been there for the majority of the war. They haven't seen it as it's been fought in Sri Lanka, and so a popular criticism is: You left. You took your children, we're still here, we're fighting, and either you're funding this war that's killing our kids while you're safely overseas, or You're overseas, so you should support us. That can be spun any number of ways. You owe us because you got out, versus, You owe us to stop the war because you got out.

SM: Has the war affected your family?

VG: I can't think of many Sri Lankan families the war has not affected. Sure, the war has affected my family. My father in particular comes from Jaffna, and Jaffna has of course been incredibly affected by the war. My father left Sri Lanka because he anticipated this violence. But those who are really affected are those who were left behind.

SM: Do you still have relatives living there?

VG: Yes. Often I don't hear from them. I remember I mailed a letter to a cousin whose birthday it was one month, and she got the letter five months later after her birthday. And that's a pretty mild example of what I mean.

SM: How do they live there? How do your relatives actually live there? Day to day with all the bombings and the kidnappings? How do they go to school and shop for groceries? How do they do all the things that people do in cities?

VG: For them it's been that way for such a long time. I don't think that means they take it any easier, but they are not surprised, perhaps, any longer. I went to Sri Lanka last in 2005, and very shortly after that, the village that I visited was evacuated so my whole family was not there. They pick up and go when they have to. I know that one of my cousins' schools was used to house refugees. Electric current in Jaffna is very inconsistent, and one of my cousins was, I think, six years old before he ever saw electricity. There's a thousand inconveniences, and I think they just have stopped adding them up because if they did—What useful purpose would that serve? And at the same time they haven't known it to be any other way.

SM: An entire generation that's grown up knowing nothing but war.

VG: Exactly, and some of those people are my relatives. I actually went when it was relatively peaceful, just in the post-tsunami window when it was calm, and I think in different villages the security situation is different. I'm sure that if you're a girl it's probably different. For a long time in Sri Lanka, earlier, in the '80s—it was very risky for young men, because either the Tigers would recruit you or the Sri Lankan Army would assume the Tigers were recruiting you and would harass you or kidnap you or whatever, so especially to be a young person there is very risky.

SM: What's your impression of the Tamil Tigers? Now they're considered a terrorist group by the States and the European Union. And mainly people in the Tamil areas of Sri Lanka and among the Tamil diaspora—not just Sri Lankan Tamils but also Indian Tamils consider them freedom fighters. What's your impression of this group?

VG: That's one of the things the book tries to address and says that you can choose to be a moderate in that battle. It's an unfortunate situation. The Tigers at their very beginnings had and still have some legitimate grievances against a government that commits human rights violations. At the same time the Tigers have done incredibly horrible things . . . and have really been ruthless in saying: if you're Tamil and you don't support us, we are not going to brook any dissent. It's really sad that this political grievance has led people to do things that are morally reprehensible on both sides. If you're going to talk about it you have to acknowledge that both sides have done things that are horrifying.

SM: This is a very complicated political stew. How do you take all of this and turn it into literature? How do you deal with politics like this and have characters who are political without turning didactic, which your novel clearly is not? How do you pull that off?

VG: It was really hard, and there are certainly things I wish I could have included that somehow didn't fit. If it wasn't organic to the narrative, it didn't necessarily happen. The family in the book is a Jaffna Tamil family, and so there isn't, for example, really the voice of the Sri Lankan Muslim in the novel.

Rather than sort of pursue a political agenda, first I think that the point is to have good fiction, and if some sort of statement about morality emerges from that, that's great. But my priority was to make a story that revealed something, and I didn't necessarily want what it was revealing to be so plain.

The book was checked by a couple of PhD students in anthropology who are my friends, and I listened to them insofar as I could. And in a couple of cases they suggested that I be more specific, but for the good of the narrative, I chose not to. Maybe the point wasn't when a specific riot took place, but rather that there were riots all the time, and maybe it doesn't matter when they took place because they were so ubiquitous.

SM: And this is your first book, and obviously it's a deeply personal book because the path that your own family took is apparent in it. Novelists voyeur into invented worlds so it should not be read as biography or memoir—

VG: I hope not. [Laughs]

SM: What's your personal stake in the book? It comes through, the passion that you have, the feeling for the characters. How necessary was this book for you to write?

VG: For a book to be good, from my point of view, it has to be necessary. It was very necessary. I started writing it as my senior thesis in college, but it actually changed quite a bit after that. It started as a story that was really about a family and it became a story that was about a family in politics and a family that was choosing to be active in politics as opposed to a family that had politics happen to them. Although both elements are still in the book, and I do think that the political dilemma of the narrator is one that I personally think is important for me as someone who was born and raised in the U.S. but still, in classic *Roots* fashion, feels a responsibility to where my parents came from. It's important to engage politically. Even when it's extremely complicated. Even when it's inconvenient. Even when it's politically hairy. The more I learned about the war the more that I felt that I was compelled to say something about it, not in the voice of an activist, but in the voice of an artist.

Reading Group Questions and Topics for Discussion

1. At the beginning of the novel, Yalini befriends and then breaks off her friendship with an unnamed male. What do you think draws her to him in the first place? Why does she break off the friendship? What does the relationship tell you about her character?

2. There are several obvious doubles in the novel—Yalini and Janani, Kunju and Tharshi, Murali and Kumaran. Why do you think pairs are so important? How do these relationships compare and relate to each other? Can you think of any other significant pairs?

3. Why do you think Ganeshananthan chooses to write in fragmented vignettes?

4. Father-daughter relationships are important to this book. How does Murali and Yalini's relationship compare with Kumaran and Janani's relationship? How is Yalini's budding relationship with Kumaran different from her relationship with Murali?

5. Yalini describes her family as "globe-scattered" (3). How is setting important in the novel? What do you see as the places that are most important to Yalini's family story? How, in particular, is Toronto significant? Jaffna? America?

6. Violence plays a large part in this story—some incidents are personal, some political, and some accidental. Yalini's great-grandfather's murder, various sets of ethnic riots, the violence between Rajan and Harini, and the burns suffered by Kunju all mark milestones in the novel. How do incidents of emotional violence accomplish something similar? Do they?

7. When she meets Kumaran, Yalini becomes the unofficial family historian. Later, she says that, in order to do so, she had to learn to think in the first person. Why is it so important to Yalini to tell her family's story?

8. Why do you think Ganeshananthan chooses the title *Love Marriage*? How is it important to each of the relationships that she writes about?

9. After trying several times to stop Janani's wedding, Yalini comes to a realization. She says: "She was doing it for him, because she thought he would want to see tradition preserved, if not in the form of a Tamil country, then in the form of a Tamil daughter" (265). Do you agree with Yalini about Janani's motivations? How do they set her apart from Yalini? Do you believe that this is what Kumaran wanted for his daughter?

10. Even after the attack on the wedding site, Janani still marries Suthan. How does this choice affect or implicate Yalini in political violence?

11. At the end of the novel, Yalini asks herself whether she, if faced with the same situations as Kumaran and Janani, would have acted similarly, saying: "governments call men terrorists to erase their reason, to make them crazy. Some of them are, and some of them are not. What does that make me?" (272). How do you think Yalini comes to terms with Kumaran's actions? Do you think she too would have joined the Tigers had she not lived in America?

12. Tharshi's daughter Uma does not fit into the marriage categories that Yalini lays out on the first page. Instead, Tharshi says that her daughter was "Too Special to Get Married." Later, Yalini confesses that she has much of Uma in her. Do you think that Yalini will ever get married? Or is she, also, Too Special?

PHOTO: PRESTON MERCHANT

V. V. Ganeshananthan received her BA in 2002 from Harvard, where *Love Marriage* began as her senior thesis. She graduated from the Iowa Writers' Workshop in 2005, served for a year as the Writer in Residence at Phillips Exeter Academy, and earned an MA in journalism from Columbia University in 2007. *Love Marriage* is her first novel. She lives in New York City. Her website is www.vasugi.com